Hervé Guibert died of A[...] was one of France's m[...] novels include *To the Friend Who Did Not Save My Life*, a document of the last months of Michel Foucault, and *The Gangsters*, published by Serpent's Tail.

MY PARENTS

HERVÉ GUIBERT

translated by Liz Heron

to nobody

Library of Congress Catalog Card Number: 93-84649

A catalogue record for this book can be obtained from
the British Library on request

Copyright © 1986 by Editions Gallimard
Translation copyright © 1993 Liz Heron

The quotation on pp 63–4 from 'The Legend of St Julian of
Hospitator' from *Three Tales* by Gustave Flaubert, translated by
Robert Baldick (Penguin Classics, 1961) is reproduced by
permission of Penguin Books Ltd. Copyright © Robert Baldick,
1961.

First published in 1986 as *Mes Parents* by Editions Gallimard,
Paris
This edition first published in 1993 by
Serpent's Tail, 4 Blackstock Mews, London N4
and 401 West Broadway #1, New York, NY 10012

Typeset in 11½/15pt Bembo by Servis Filmsetting, Manchester
Printed in Great Britain by Cox & Wyman Ltd., Reading,
Berkshire

On Thursday 21 July 1983, when I am on the island of Elba and her sister Suzanne is at her country place in Gisors, my 76-year-old great-aunt Louise has a bad turn on the number 49 bus going towards the Gare du Nord, where she is to buy a train ticket in advance of some trip. She feels as if she's dying. She gets off the bus. She feels a little better. She decides she'll still go to the station and takes the metro; maybe it was the jolting motion of the bus just after lunch that made her feel sick. Yet this sense of death had never been so definite or intense. A new idea takes firm shape in her mind, a conviction. When she gets home she stops on the second-floor landing and turns the key which is still in the lock of Suzanne's apartment door. The apartment is empty, the shutters are closed, and in the gloom the heat has abated; she dabs at her over-moist brow. She knows she has to do the job quickly if she is to forestall any scruples or allow her reluctance to prevail. This pious woman behaves like a vandal. One by one she yanks out the drawers of Suzanne's desk, dog-earing fragile bundles of papers, crumpling them in her agitation as she scans them, putting to one side those that seem compromising, flies into a rage at not finding the ones she's obsessed with, and comes across Suzanne's travel diaries, where her eyes quickly alight upon some obscenity; these she adds to the condemned items, runs like a Fury to the massive wardrobe in the bedroom and, it's as if she's doing battle with the dresses, when she clutches at an old one a flap of silk comes away in her hand while the shoulders stay clamped to the hanger; and it is at last in the small drawer at the back, which she knew was there, but whose secrets she had never gone so far as to violate, that she finds those particular papers – filth that must go the way of filth – and without bothering to ascertain exactly what they say, their resonating memory being already too shameful, she piles them on top of the travel diaries and goes up to the third floor to burn them in the stove.

She is tired, experiencing for the first time both guilt and the sense of duty honoured.

When, still on Elba, I call Suzanne, now back from Gisors, to hear her news, I can tell from her voice that she is upset; she tells me what Louise has done, Louise whom she has always trusted. When I get back I ply her with questions. I am well aware that she doesn't want to tell me what those papers were. I insist. She asks me: 'Do you love your mother?' Of course I don't answer. 'Then you shouldn't be told,' she says, 'your poor mother is so ill I can't do that to her.' I tell her that what one imagines is always more dreadful than the truth. 'Then imagine that your mother is a fiend, a vampire, a succubus,' she tells me.

On the eighth of September I go to celebrate Suzanne's birthday, in Gisors, where she has returned. In the garden, sitting in her rattan easy chair after lunch, she talks of blame and punishment, of retribution and expiation; she who is no Christian. This brings us back to my mother's dastardly deed, which she still does not want to tell me about. I tell her I'm fond of scandal. She says: 'Then you'll be the one to write the book I couldn't write about the scandal.' I ask her if it was one of their dogs that my mother sinned with, I ask her the name of the victims occasioned by her deed, she tells me that there were no victims, but, with extreme disgust, that it was simply foul. She says she will tell me about it when I get back from Mexico . . .

At 29 – the age I am now as I begin this story – my father is living in Nice; he has a veterinary practice, two horses, a green Ford, a sailing boat, and is engaged to a young *bourgeoise*. To the person who narrates this to me thirty-five years later Uncle Raoul recounts that he is in a rush to buy himself a dress coat for the wedding. A few months later my father abruptly left Nice; then he is back in Paris, without a change of socks, sponging off his mother, with a job at the Sécurité Sociale, resuming his medical studies.

At the very same time my mother, who is studying to be an optician, has fallen in love with the parish priest at Courlandon; she steals money from her aunt to give to him; she has her sister Gisèle and her cousin Micheline go with her on their bicycles to the presbytery; the two accomplices stand look-out while my mother hands over whatever cash she has managed to scrounge in exchange for the priest's embraces.

To the aunt who took her in as a child, the little black-clad orphan whose father had drowned himself in the canal inside his car, my mother confesses that she is pregnant by the parish priest. My great-aunt Suzanne, who experiences this episode as a most shameful thing, dares not tell her husband and confides instead in one of her violinist friends, Suzanne, who is my father's aunt. The two Suzannes agree to strike a fast bargain to reintroduce the two young people who had met in their childhood when my father was fifteen and my mother eight years old.

Scarcely a month later a meeting is arranged at the office of my mother's aunt and uncle, who are pharmacists. My father's aunt Suzanne is there too. My mother informs her uncle that she is pregnant by a young man called Serge. At the same time my father demands fourteen million francs: he wants to set himself up as a vet again and buy a clinic on avenue Mozart. The uncle vilifies the man who could become his son-in-law (he has always regarded my mother as his daughter): 'You're just a good-for-nothing, a crook, make yourself scarce! We won't be needing you to bring up Jeannine's child . . .' My mother bursts into sobs and drags my father, who is indeed on the point of flight, up to the top floor of the house, where she begs him to stay: 'You'll have the money, I swear to you!' – 'How will you do it?' my father asks. 'I'll blackmail them,' my mother retorts, 'they've got gold they came by illegally, either they give it to us or else we'll report them!' My mother and father marry on the 28th of April 1951, five months before the birth of my sister, Dominique.

When I get back from Mexico, Suzanne comes out with the whole story: the love story between my mother and the parish priest, her pregnancy, the machinations of the two women friends to marry off their niece and nephew before they even meet, the blackmail for the money, the threats of exposure. She tells me that my father is a gangster, a ne'er-do-well, and that was why he had to get out of Nice fast like someone unsavoury; wielding the same kind of blackmail, knocking up a young girl from a good family so as to get money out of her. But the scam went awry and that's why my father ended up losing all he owned. So I must have a half-brother in Nice, as has sometimes been hinted at in things my father has said. What's more, my sister isn't my sister, but my half-sister, the parish priest's child. My parents married lovelessly. This gets Suzanne going: 'For you're Jewish you know, you are Jews.' I'm flabbergasted; my father has always made a point of having nothing to do with Jews. Suzanne is emphatic: 'You are Jewish, anyway your father had to get away from the Germans, because he had his mother's name, Neethofer, which is a Jewish name; his father, Lucien Guibert, hadn't acknowledged him and it was only much later that he was able to take the name that he hadn't been given; Guibert isn't your real name – and another proof of your Jewishness: he had you circumcised.' At that point I am compelled mentally to look down at my prick and check that my glans is indeed covered by its foreskin. Louise adds a detail: 'You're circumcised, I remember, when you were small one day I went to your house and you told me you had a little sore place and you wanted to show me . . .' Something about this story is not right.

My parents move in with my father's aunt, Suzanne Logeart, who has lived alone in her flat at 68 rue Michel-Ange ever since her husband Raoul died in a

sanatorium. My father borrows money from Boby –
the boyfriend of his other aunt, Geneviève – who lives
in Tananarive, where he manages a cocoa plantation.
This man realizes that he's going blind and he sits down
on the beach by the sea and fires a bullet into his temple
with his rifle; Suzanne tells me that my father rubbed his
hands together because he didn't have to pay him back.
With the money he buys x-ray equipment and takes
over his aunt's kitchen, her office and part of her living-
room to do duty as a vet's surgery. He puts up a plaque
outside. My mother stands in as his secretary and
assistant, putting on a white overall for the job of
holding the dogs' paws and taking off their muzzles.
Clients are infrequent though sometimes prestigious
(Brigitte Bardot, Prince Ioussoupov who killed Raspu-
tin; when I am a child these names of my father's clients
will be fabled echoes), and many do not pay their bills.
My father falls prey to a terrible obsession which at first
he keeps secret: contamination by radiation from the x-
ray equipment. Every month he goes to Villejuif
hospital to have his blood and his lungs checked.
However much care he takes wearing gloves and
making sure that his limbs are not caught in the
radiation beam, he has no option but to hold the animal
against the screen. When his fixation is at its peak he sees
the whole apartment as contaminated by the x-rays;
everything from the armchairs down to his wife's hair,

is steeped in radioactive matter. He goes to the Ministry of Public Works to put in his application for a post as a veterinary inspector. The radiation and the erratic nature of his clients' payments have got the better of him. He's afraid. He wants a son.

My sister is born on the 26th of September 1951. A short time later my father begins work at Police Headquarters; he gets an official card. Any sign of bother with an officer and he will say in an undertone: 'I'm with the firm,' his voice emphatic and complicit. It's at this time that he makes an application for municipal housing at the central office of the Paris HLM: he's on a low civil servant's salary with a daughter to bring up and a wife not working. For months on end he turns up at their offices bleating, shabbily dressed expressly to achieve his purpose, flattering or greasing the palm of some other civil servant as needs be. Finally my parents and my sister move house, into a three-room flat with kitchen and bathroom on the sixth floor of 52 rue de l'Amiral Mouchez, a street whose distinguishing feature is that it straddles the thirteenth and the fourteenth arrondissements; a yellow brick building with red columns, pretty ugly but not too bad for an HLM, with two windows overlooking the street and two on to the back courtyard, due south just as my father wanted.

★

The only memory I can have of those three years of family life spent without me is through the sixteen millimetre black and white films my father shot with his Uncle Raoul's Paillard camera, which I still have. My sister has a slightly hooked nose and with her tomboyish ways it isn't long before she splits her forehead on a stone balustrade; she will always have that vertical scar, right between her eyebrows, which she will hide with her fringe. Christmases are spent at Ezanville, with my father's mother and grandmother, Alice Fortoul and Eugénie Neethofer (there's a rift with my mother's family at the time); holidays at Croix-de-Vie, where my parents have found a little place to rent with a fishing family, the Coutuis. For a while they'll play at being monied, philanthropic city-slickers, coming back year after year with boxes full of old clothes and cast-off toys. Which makes me frequently aware that what lies against my skin and absorbs its sweat and is chafed threadbare against it will soon go on to clothe that of my little alter ego in the Vendée, who is just a little older than me and who will always have garments that are too short, since I wear them the right size for me, and this gives me an inkling of my parents' smug superiority, and their pity, while feeling a certain luxuriant disgust that is less explicable. At Croix-de-Vie my father already has a sailing boat; on days when there's a high wind he takes my mother with him and has her bail out.

I am born at dawn on the 14th December 1955, and — either because of clinic vacancies or loyalty to some midwife – at Saint-Cloud, on a site, my mother tells me, now traversed by cars on a motorway. In my cradle then in my bed I am swaddled in a voluminous white woollen garment, soiled and all fluff-balls, turned round so often it was hard to say where the hood was; this is my cape, its stitching worn away by my gums. It enfolds me, I encase myself in it, I clean myself with it, I melt into it, lick it, suck it, rub myself with it, I disappear beneath it, I love being smothered in its nappy, pappy smell; I gnaw at it greedily and it shreds, and the more ruined it is the more I love it, the more I cling on to it and howl when anyone tries to take it from me, holding out a brand new cape that stinks of cleanness; though I do not know it, these are my last nights of crazy love with this cape and it is in my tummy that I should hide it and save it since it has served me so well as a tummy, my little flat woolly twin, the two of us embracing clamped together, me pissing on it and it laughing, and one morning I wake up dreadfully naked, my skin raw to the quick with that skin cut away; I don't howl now, I am solemn, perhaps I have guessed that it's gone into the rubbish chute, scrunched up and thrown down from the sixth floor on top of kitchen scraps and the burst dustbags of vacuum cleaners; I am told it's just been taken to Madame Hélène, the laundress, and I can go and fetch it myself all lovely and clean; I go, and the laundress, who's in on the plot, hands me a fake plastic bag with the new shawl I had rejected; I won't degrade my fingers or my sleep with it, I don't take it. My first notion of death, my first contempt.

Images can get hellishly under your skin. Without giving a thought to the look of it, my parents crudely tacked up reproductions of two quite famous paintings, torn from the pages of magazines: Van Gogh's café terrace one summer night in Arles, an almost abstract image of the soft heat, of deliquescence, of vacancy, of summer (and prefiguring the pleasure with which my adult body would acquaint me), and Munch's *Scream*, altered, through the slow disfigurement of an already disfigured human form, into an image of fear and death. The way in which these two images irradiate my infant body is so intense that I schooled myself to blindness whenever I went past them. Quickly, they return to their condition of magazine pages vitiated by poor quality print, shoddy flat surfaces with spurious colours. When they have become scorched and yellowed by the heat from a radiator, pitted with drawing-pin marks, they too are thrown down the rubbish chute.

Once, my parents sedulously tell me, there were Germans who tortured French people; they say it as if they were the ones who were tortured, and they spare nothing in their description of this torture: French people roughly awakened as they sleep the sleep of the hungry, and taken, tied up together like animals, to a big room whose walls and floor are lined with metal, and packed in there. Then the room is locked and the floor begins to get hot; the men and women climb on top of one another to escape from burning, for they've been taken there with bare hands and feet; they trample one another underfoot trying to climb up the walls in this windowless room, but by now the ceiling too is red hot. The Nazis hidden on the other side of the doors savour the aroma of roasted flesh wafting out along with the prayers.

My father leaves early in the morning for the slaughter-houses, which are still at les Halles, breakfasting alone as he listens to the radio and leaving us a note on the kitchen table when there is something special, most memorably: 'Kennedy has been assassinated', 'Edith Piaf is dead'. Suddenly he's picking his way past puddles of blood, now deaf to the screams of the animals being dragged or pushed towards the pistol or the blade, and on some good-humoured mornings he makes up music in his head from all this bellowing; he puts on a white overall, checks that his rubber stamps are there in his pocket, puts on his glasses to go and inspect the carcasses, stamps them, and 'does the glands' with an incision. When he gets home in the afternoon sometimes he brings, wrapped in newspaper, a brain or an ox tongue that he has been given in exchange for a dodgy customs clearance. They have to be eaten. Once when my sister and I are being made to swallow calf's sweetbreads, my father puts his watch on the table and gives us five minutes to finish up what's on our plates: blows come thick and fast, we vomit the white marrow and have to chew it all over again along with our tears and our snot.

To begin with I sleep in my sister's room. My earliest memories are of nightmares waking me up and making me fight against sleep so as to avoid confronting them, sitting up in bed waiting for daylight. I already have Pet Lamb with me; I was told that I got him for my first birthday. He's a little white lamb with a flower on his pink nose which I soon pulled off, and I started dressing him in my sister's dolls' clothes: sweaters and ski-pants, but dresses too and bathing costumes, for every year I take him to the seaside. My sister, reminiscing about this period with me the other day, was still complaining that I swiped her dolls' clothes and that I would always frighten her by hiding in the shadow of her wardrobe – something which really amazed me because I had a memory of myself as a very fearful little boy. One day my sister gets a present of a doll's dress whose sleeves and hem are trimmed with angora: I finger this prickly wool which is extravagantly softer and without the static that mohair has but with all its cunning sensuousness. As I finger this substance, for the first time, there and then, I fall to dreaming of some day rubbing it or even just putting it on top of my prick, which is, I know all too well, the most sensitive part of my body. Already I'm in the habit – and it's a daring one, for my mother's always busy in the next room – of opening my trousers to caress my prick with something unusual: the curly fleece of a paint roller that's lying around, and which even today can turn me on when I see or touch the jacket or just the lapel lining of a sheepskin. As a child I never managed to get hold of that little scrap of angora that I would have liked to cut off – the hem of the dress – to decorate my prick with. But what was meant to be a dining-room is turned into my bedroom and then, as compensation, I can pinch my mother's balls of knitting wool, set them, as if inadvertently, next to my bed, and when the light is turned out hold my breath and slip the ball of wool between the sheets and fondle my sex with it. It is then too, when I must be about four or five, that in a dream I picture some kind of place of pleasure, a stovepipe grey colour, where men strip naked and each take their place in a stall where fire excites their senses, the flames licking at their sexual parts.

I go to the school in rue de la Tombe-Issoire. The earliest memory I have of this school is the arrival one afternoon of a musical group which consisted I think of two people: possibly a man playing a musical saw but for sure there was a woman in a long dress playing the harp. It's the first time I see people perform and, sitting there on a wooden bench, I'm bowled over. I remember too the taste of the liquorice we put in the pitchers to change the colour of the water, and those tubes or little round, flat metal boxes filled with their yellow powder. On one day a week only, instead of this water, there is a bottle of chocolate milk, a real treat. One of the big boys, a red-haired one, catches me and, holding me tight against him, runs to the toilets and locks me inside in the darkness with him. I am pressed against his chest, or his throat, which has a warm odour of ginger-haired sweat and rank wool; he's wearing a heavy-knit V-necked pullover that's dirty and shapeless and gaudily coloured. From the wool that clings hotly to his torso I drink in this smell with my heart beating fast; sucking at it I'm in ecstasy. The next morning at breakfast I boast about this incident; my sister whines about it to my mother, who is busy polishing shoes, and she takes fright: 'Hervé, you are not to follow the big boys into the toilets, it's not nice, this boy must be a pervert . . .' If I'm four then, the big boy must be about six or seven. His name is Christian and everyone knows that he does that, taking the little boys into the toilets and locking himself in with them, hugging them in the shitty darkness, doing nothing else. I don't let him take me again, but I dress up Pet Lamb in a V-necked pullover just like the one that gave me so much pleasure, and I call Pet Lamb Christian, or else darling.

My father often leaves for the weekend to go sailing with friends and soon he'll buy a share in a sailing boat that will be christened at Le Havre. When he gets home it's not blood he smells of as he usually does, but salt. This is when my mother talks to her aunt about divorce. We often wind up on our own with her. She has a strange habit when she gets annoyed, when we exasperate her, of saying she's going to leave us and go and live in Cuba. Why Cuba? I have long reflected on this name that both scares me and promises so many delights: an enchanted jail where you drink coconut milk through a straw. Along with my sister I have always surmised there was a man hidden behind this name: a daring bearded warrior, a sea wolf far fiercer than our father. But there was nothing behind this name, we realized: one day in the heat of her anger my mother bids us a solemn farewell and announces that this time it's for real, she's off to Cuba. My sister and I pull back the living room curtains to watch her disappear round a street corner. We don't panic. We believed her but we go on living as if she were with us. Two hours later she comes back, unembarrassed, as if nothing had happened and without any explanation; she has a new hairdo, she went to the hairdresser to calm down. My sister and I are more disappointed than relieved. From that day on my mother never mentions Cuba, as if she really had gone there. Her new destination is Nouméa.

Often while we're eating this grotesque sequence takes place before us across the sixth floor window; first a hand, then an arm, then a ponytail, then the face of a little girl who has lost all fear of hanging there on the void by her feet and the good offices of her father, having got thoroughly on his nerves it would seem, and who starts clowning about and sending us secret sign language. The father's nerves are in truth slightly shot; Monsieur Fimpontel is back from the war in Algeria and there are nights when he gets up and hits the radiators with an iron bar and all the strength he can muster.

Sometimes we go on holiday to Ezanville, to the house of my father's mother, Alice Fortoul. The day begins to seem very strange; our father hasn't showed his face since morning; we can't get into the kitchen, for the door is permanently shut; we quiz our mother: our father is in a bad mood; an upset we cannot be told about has made him hole up in this kitchen from which he won't budge. Can we at least talk to him through the door? It would be better if we went to play in the garden. Our capering around in the grass suddenly becomes something anxious and restrained as if it was drawing us towards the kitchen window, though it was on the other side of the house, where we were no longer supposed to go that day. Suddenly, without any explanation, my mother comes to fetch my sister. I go on jumping about in the grass, getting more and more anxious; despite her promise, my sister does not come back. The silent house, its doors and windows closed, shadowless behind the curtains, has become threatening. My mother comes to fetch me in turn, taking me up to the kitchen door and telling me I'm going to see my father again now. She gives a curt knock and right away the door opens and my mother pushes me inside the kitchen where my father grabs me, taking hold of my arms and slipping them into the sleeves of a back-to-front smock which he then ties; he himself wears a white smock and my mother puts one on too; there's a horrid smell of ether which gives me nasty shivers. My father has a syringe in his hand, my mother presses me against her and with one hand tries to blindfold my panic-stricken eyes and with the other to stifle my screams while my father gives me the injection. Then, in tears,

I'm taken up to our room, where I find my sister, who has also been given the injection, in a furious state. For my parents, putting on this act for us, stabbing us in the back, lying, this whole elaborate ruse had been preferable, or else cheaper, than the standard visit to a doctor's surgery.

The top right-hand drawer in my sister's desk can be locked. One day, looking for something, my mother finds the key and in the drawer discovers a diary my sister keeps which refers, without a shadow of a doubt, to an attempted poisoning of my parents. In this hazardous venture she has an accomplice, a girl called Laurence, of whom we have never heard before and who must be the one who supplied her with the poison (her father is a chemist). Pronto, hopping mad (those are her own expressions), my mother takes herself off to the lycée Montaigne and waits for playtime to corner my sister and her evil pal; but though she goes all over the playground she can't find my sister, or rather she can't recognize her, until the point when she realizes that one particular body with its back always turned to her and all got up in remarkably fancy style is in a no less remarkable panic because of her being there. The fact is that my sister, who must be twelve years old, is unrecognizable. While my mother does her utmost to dress her like a nice little girl – flat shoes, kilts, blazers –

there she is in stockings, stiletto-heeled shoes and wearing lipstick, got up like a real slut. The game was up: my sister arrives at the lycée in her family outfit then dashes into one of the toilet cubicles where all her tart's paraphernalia is stashed on top of the cistern. She changes in the morning and changes back in the evening and nobody notices a thing. My mother washes my sister's face under a tap, rips her stockings to pieces and doles out threats to the unspeakable Laurence, who is of course the one responsible for these perversions. My sister will be banned from seeing her.

Early one winter morning, it's still dark, the first snow lit by the street lamps, turning it almost blue. As we do every morning, we go a little way down rue de l'Amiral-Mochez then left into rue Gazan where the *Echo de la Mode* is, with the gorgeous dress patterns in the windows, and climb the stairs leading to a platform in front of the parc Montsouris, where we catch the number 21 bus. After climbing the steps more slowly than usual we come out onto the slippery esplanade and the snow is really blue, or very yellow, and the park will be closed. My mother's gloves hold my gloves or as frequently happens I haven't wanted to put any on and against my palm I have this smooth almost moist black contact of the leather. And just then there's some kind of rapid confused movement which I can't quite reconstruct but whose outcome alas I can see quite clearly: has one of the three of us slipped? Have we just missed the bus? Quickly my mother takes off her glove, pulls a handkerchief out of her bag, spits on it and rubs my lips with it. It reeks. The breath of a woman who has fasted since last night, mixed with an aroma of snow or that decoction of perfumes that wafts out of the bag as soon as the clasp is snapped open: lipstick, tiny liquorice parma violets, the paper photographs are printed on, sundry sweet debris. It is unforgettable.

I've already mentioned it in the sweetbreads episode; our father beats us up, particularly my sister. Once because she stole a television pencil sharpener in the bookshop on avenue Reille. Another time because she lies; my parents found the lie out easily; my sister said she was going to visit the Observatory, but my parents suspect her of still going out with the accursed Laurence. On a hunch my father goes downstairs to ring the Observatory from the telephone kiosk, and they tell him it's only open on the first Saturday of every month. When my sister gets home my mother asks her: 'Well was the Observatory good?' – 'Terrific,' my sister answers, and there and then my father – who is waiting in the hallway like a maddened animal – pulls his belt off his trousers and whiplashes it in the air and shoves my sister into her room, shutting them firmly in together.

My mother and I hear the blows and, weeping, I beg her to put an end to them. We are often beaten with the strap that my mother bought at the hardware shop; with the first one, then the second one, for we tried to get rid of it in the rubbish chute before blocking the toilet with it, which earned us a hiding with the thongs wetted. Once, in my room, my father hits me too hard and dislocates my jaw; I'm left feeling a complete idiot, unable to say another word. Almost following through the movement of the blow, my father knocks my jaw back in place with a sharp punch under my chin.

It's as if my parents have divided up the ownership of my body. At seven, when my mother wakes me, my father has already left for work; it is she who gets me up, dresses me, feeds, me, takes me to the toilet then wipes my bottom. She will still be wiping it when I'm twelve. Every Sunday she washes me under the shower – we have a small slipper-bath where you can't stretch out – she soaps me, draws the shower curtain, makes me rinse the soap off and I'm supposed to call her when it's all washed away; she goes back to the kitchen to get on with her chores and often in this interval I start jerking off and what sweet torture it is to make myself come fast enough so that I can call her back without arousing her suspicion. She'll go on washing me like that until I'm thirteen. Then I sit on a towel laid out on my bed and my mother twists little balls of cotton wool onto a stick to clean out my ears with, then she moistens one with eau de Cologne to do my navel, so tickly it's almost painful.

In the evening I must give myself up into my father's hands. On ordinary days as the afternoon draws in I am in my room reading after finishing my homework, my mother is preparing dinner and invariably my mother and father can be heard shouting certain stock phrases across the apartment: 'Did you put water in the humidifiers?', then: 'Wash your hands. Sit down at the table!' just like at a boarding school. I'm always last, so they call me from the kitchen: 'Hervelino!'; I love that moment. While we're eating we listen to the Duraton Family with Zappy Max on the radio. After the fruit course my father and I leave the table to play a game we've invented for our mutual entertainment: I stand barefoot on top of his feet, or rather on his Turkish slippers, tucking my head into his tummy so as I can't see anything, and my stiff, uncoordinated puppet's legs follow the movements of his legs pulling them like strings, my father leading me into the most shadowy nooks and crannies of the apartment, which is now all in darkness (lights are never left on except when people are in the room), losing me. When he stops I have to guess where he has brought me. Then he switches on the light and I am just as happy whether I've won or lost and ask to start all over again, but it's time for hands to be washed again, with nails scraped well into the soap to eliminate the microbes of the meal; then teeth: Gingiva Spécia toothpaste. Then from the bathroom my father brings the cotton wool and the bottle of eau de Cologne, decanted once a week out of the big bottle with a funnel, and takes me into my room where I get up and stand fully dressed on my bed. My father undresses me very slowly, slipping my trousers off all the way down the tops of my legs while I hang on to his neck, then my underpants, then getting me to lift one leg at a time to put on my pyjama trousers – this is when I can play at not wanting to lift my leg so as to make the pleasure of it last. Then I stretch out on my bed, which is where my father sits with a towel laid across his knees for my feet to rest on and he soaks little balls of cottonwool in eau de Cologne and dabs them over and over between each of my toes; in this exquisite pleasure my father's studied movements modulate my sighs. Neither my mother nor my sister are allowed to play any part in this, nor even to be there. Then, with my playing at being as helpless as a laundry bundle, my father lifts me up in his arms, lays me down, tucks me in tight as can be and gives me a kiss. He has put out the light and is standing up against my bed, making me say my prayers out loud: an Our Father, then a Hail Mary. One sleepless night last summer I try to summon up the words and they seem simultaneously absurd, abstract and thoroughly solemn: flimflam about kingdom come and holiness, but rediscovered they are, words I would think I'd never ever heard if I did not know for sure that I'd repeated them hundreds of times, and that night I'm immensely touched by them: 'Forgive us our trespasses as we forgive those who trespass against us', 'now and at the hour of our death, Amen'. These words could easily have been replaced by some pornographic litany, given that for my father, as his bedtime ritual, they were just a way of yoking voices together, a coupling of breath.

There are hairdresser days. The back of my head has had all that it can take of the iron shears of the hairdresser in rue de l'Amiral-Mouchez with its shopfront of washed out turquoise tiles. My father takes me to the most chic hairdresser in rue de Tolbiac, a man who looks like Taras Boulba but who does women's hair when he's not at the till and I am entrusted to a grey-skinned employee of faintly indeterminate sex, who might well work as a waiter in a station buffet and who is sometimes seen about wearing a little fur collar: to think twenty years later, when I'd completely forgotten about him, his face comes back to me with perfect clarity. In the mirror my father keeps an eye on every single move he makes; in an imperious tone he has ordered a razor cut – it costs a thousand francs – answering the usual question with:

'Short, very short,' and with my always adding: 'Not too short.' I hate going to the hairdresser, it feels as if my hair is being murdered. To get me there my father first takes me window shopping round the Paquebot Normandie, the toyshop next door; from what's at eye-level I select a medieval lady in a coif, a plaster-cast falconer with tight-fitting breeches, a jester with bells, or a wounded soldier from the Second World War. They are not bought right away; my father promises I'm to have one, but only after the haircut, so long as I don't make too much fuss. With the talcum powder fresh on the back of my neck absorbing the cheap eau de Cologne which only irritates it all the more, I go into the toyshop, which is deliciously dark and odorous: boxes, balls of string, modelling plasticine, the rustle of the drabbest smocks in the whole world (those of Monsieur and Madame Valtonet), the fresh paint of squeaking masks, fire-cracker powder, ribbons trailing, the new rubber of tricycle wheels.

Marbles, I like them so much and I've won so many of them that I could fill my mouth and my whole intestinal tract with them and just be a little man made of marbles; I've got several sets of them that I tip into a shoe box at night. When it isn't the season for marbles I look at them with a certain sadness. I can't wait for the scoubidou season and the paper cut-out season to be over, then I hurl myself back into the fray. I have become the marbles ace, I'm the one who started playing for a hundred, a stroke of genius; my rivals only play for ten. Every morning I go out with an empty container, a half-full container and in my pockets some big marbles that count for ten. I've got my pitch reserved just to the right of the door between the covered part of the playground and the yard; right beside the wall the asphalt has a tiny egg cup-shaped scoop in it which seems specially made to hold my marbles. I have my patch which I pay for with marbles, and I have my workers to keep an eye on the players. I work out the distance that has to be covered for a particular win; it has to make the marble virtually invisible. The marbles come thick and fast and I check that my little marble hasn't moved, steadying it so that it won't. At the same time my workers collect the marbles and fill up one of my two containers lying open on the ground with me hardly bothering to watch them – I pay them too well. Nobody beats me. When my two containers and all my pockets are full to the brim and my workers' pockets are also pretty full, I remove my lovely marble. Before I go I always give away some marbles to pacify those who have thrown away everything in this crazy performance; I hurl handfuls of marbles as far as I can and make them run after them. I like the way they're grateful to me after that.

From the Paquebot Normandie my sister and I get dozens of rolls of crêpe paper, that thin, ridged paper that you can fold easily and which comes in the boldest colours: pure pinks, greens and yellows. We roll them out, cut them up, trample on them and with them we make dresses, hats, giant cigarettes, Sioux teepees. One Sunday afternoon we put on a little song and dance show; the door frame separating my parents' rooms and mine did duty as the proscenium arch; on the other side we had set out a row of chairs, and the ugly folding door made of hideous mock leather which my parents put up as a last resort in our little Eden, to poison me with their intimacy, will be the curtain. We put on our make-up in the wings and where the audience can't see it I've got my record player with *The Nutcracker* or *Petrushka* playing and I've got all the different lamps in the flat lighting up this little space of my room. The show begins and I am the star dancer and my sister is the ballerina; we weigh nothing now, we fly through the air, the power to turn yourself into a feather is one of the triumphs of childhood.

There is one thing you can do that is more magical than anything else, even more than growing broadbeans or lentils in damp cotton wool. It is when you take some crumpled paper, an old banknote, a dog-eared picture, a message screwed up deep in your pocket and you make it new again. You put this precarious object flat on the table between two sheets of blotting paper that you have moistened just a little and you turn on the iron so that it is only slightly warm, then without pressing on it you iron the flat, pink wallet thing in which the miracle is concealed. The image which emerges is not new, but even more amazing still it is like new: the little disfiguring crack across it hasn't gone altogether, there's still a marvellous trace of it which becomes the secret which you will delight in sharing with the image.

How I love pictures; the ones I'm given at school when I've accumulated ten points for good behaviour, that wondrous currency of model conduct that turns the schoolboy into a little shareholder of his hypocrisy. The little images of history or wildlife, the saints devoured by lions, animals of the most outlandish kind: the tapir, the sapajou. But the ones I like even more are the picture cards, nicely coloured, that Préval butter puts in their cartons of the salted variety between the glistening packaging and the thin rippled paper in which the block of butter is wrapped; they represent the kings of France, who are all either pretty as a picture or ugly as fiends, with sly, pointy-faced greyhound looks, haemophiliac pallor, wearing poisoners' hats and ermine doublets and smelling deliciously of butter. On the back a biographical note details this sovereign's brief cruel passage through the gallery of kings, which makes him all the more adorable.

I have a little printing set for figures, another one for insects, another for mammals, the giraffe's neck so long that it's hard to get it all on the paper at once, but the scarab beetle is splendid, absolutely clear, like the shadow of a real scarab. I put my nose right up against the ink pad to sniff its musty violet smell while in the next room my father, wearing earphones, has his radio set crackling away; he built it himself so as, I imagine to myself, to make contact with his pilot friends in the Resistance.

When I'm five my parents take me to a Sunday matinée at the Châtelet to see *White Horse Inn* with reduced price tickets that my sister got at school; I'm bowled over. By these actors who aren't just puppets, by the commotion of set changes, by the dusty, chaotic to-ing and fro-ing which sends up clouds of powder, by the clumsy whispering of the extras, by the orchestra, by its conductor's baton and black dress suit – a certain Félix Novulone – by the faces and the smell and the feel of the programme's pages, by the scene-change pulleys that raise the sets before our eyes and by the revolving stage, by a singing child and a fat man, by the entrance of a white horse then a steamboat, by the voices, by the

depths of the stage, by the lacy decolletages that show
off the women's breasts; I'm intoxicated, knocked out
with pleasure, I want it to go on and on. I fell in love
with the Châtelet; for five years I collect tickets and
programmes, look things up in books and buy operetta
records and in the summer when *L'Aurore* finally
publishes the new season's programme that I've been
waiting for so impatiently, the title of the new show
makes me start fantasizing. One after the other there's
The Lightning Polka, the *Vienna Waltzes*, *Mediterranean*,
Monsieur Carnaval. I develop a crush on Georges
Guétary and out of loyalty to him I refuse to go and see
Luis Mariano. I try to get hold of the dresses of the
singers Nicole Broissin and Annie Duparc so I can wear
them myself. One day in my great-aunt's pharmacy the
saleswoman who gave me a fantastic blotter with a devil
on it in body-hugging green tights, spitting flames and
pressing a poultice against his torso as if it was giving
him ecstasies – and which was maybe what lay behind
that dream of the pleasure rooms where people go for
fire – this Madame Georgette gives me a sample bar of
soap and I take the paper off and, like a mirage, its aroma
brings to my nostrils the whole of the old red and gold
Châtelet hall with its dusty purple seats; it's the very
same smell that's released when I push down the
numbered seat in the centre of the front row – the one I
always ask for – to sit down. I keep this bar of soap in its

wrapping like a treasure and every now and then, when the date of the next show circled on the calendar opposite my bed (which I use to fall asleep by even more than with the thought of holidays) is too far off, I take the paper off it and inhale its smell avidly, taking care not to scratch it so that it never gets any smaller.

Holidays are quite a palaver. The evening before we set out we have to have a fight with our father so that the time for getting up isn't too early. My father always cuts discussion short by announcing categorically that the alarm will go off at five o'clock and he'll be the first to wash and dress, then he'll wake us up at half-past five and the car has to be fully loaded at half-past six and we have to be on our way absolutely no later than seven o'clock. We finish up leftovers at dinner. The luggage is already packed and in the hallway, on one side what's to go in the boot, on the other what's to be roped to the roof rack, and then what we'll get stiff legs from having between our feet. Bedtime has to be earlier than usual. My father gets virtually no sleep, at the last moment he has taken it upon himself to set the alarm for four o'clock, but he gets up at three, shaves, tunes the radio to the only programme that's on and shakes us awake at half-past three. The nightmare begins. The official reason is so as to avoid the pile-ups and heavy traffic as everyone else sets out on holiday. The secret reason is to save money on a night in a hotel. With the little red Dauphine, then the big blue Simca, between the cars' limitations and my father's caution, it easily takes us from twenty to twenty-four hours to get to the South. Around six in the evening, after twelve hours on the road, cramped and sweaty, our stomachs churned raw, starving and dispirited, ghastly pale in the rear-view mirrors – my sister having thrown up several times by the roadside despite numerous Nautamines – and my mother in the front seat, her shrieks more than once having saved my father from a memorable accident, for the tenth time we all make a show of believing that we are looking for a hotel to spend the night in. It has to be cheap, have a set menu, and not be too noisy, all of which make such a find out of the question on the evening of the first of July. Darkness has fallen, we are pale and famished and keep getting lost on little roads that might take us to improbable country inns. My father parks the car on a gravelled terrace, the headlights illuminate the blackness of his trousers, then he's gone, a dog barks, a doorbell rings a little way off and there begins a long anxious period of waiting, filled with the hope of release. Is my father discussing the price of a room? Sometimes the four of us will sleep in two beds or just one, but more often than not we'll see him come back across the headlights with a thumbnail jammed between his teeth, which means bad news, that there are no rooms left, or they're too expensive, and does our father lie to us? Sometimes he brings us little snacks and we eat them either dolefully or in a gleefully festive mood. We're on our way again. We know we've got another twelve or fifteen hours to go, that my father will wind up exhausted and so drowsy that he has to pull the car over onto a verge and sleep against the wheel, that my mother will be in tears, that the next afternoon we'll reach the Côte d'Azur and we'll have to thank our father for getting us there safe and sound. My sister is given more Nautamine. Over and over we've whiled away the time counting the caravans or noting nationalities on car numberplates so often that we are now at a loss as the night stretches before us. There's no radio in the car. My father starts singing, kind of warbling, Tino Rossi style. It's always the same song, a lovely, very mournful one: '*C'est la cloche du vieux manoir, du vieux manoir, qui sonne le retour du soir, le retour du soir*' . . . In the middle of the night a village hall of some kind looms out of the darkness on the roadside with the isolated unreality of an apparition; the merrymakers have just left and a caretaker is locking up. My father has a bright idea; he stops the car and goes over to the caretaker with a five franc bribe and a sob story, pointing out the three bundles all huddled up dead to the world behind the windscreen. He has borrowed the caretaker's torch and comes and shines it in our faces to wake us up – we have to hurry, the caretaker has other things to do, then there is all the luggage to shift out of the car, you never know. In the big empty hall lit only by the nightlight my father looks for a spot to stretch out the only duvet we have, shoving back a table, shifting a couple of chairs, edging away a pile of confetti with his foot and, after all this, dusting the floor clean with the palm of his hand. We huddle together under the duvet. My father has opted for the platform. I fall asleep again, happy as I watch the spangled, gilded fittings of a bass drum glimmer in the semi-darkness.

It is evening again, the last few kilometres no longer arduous as we coast along in anticipation of arrival; the heat is less fierce; there are bends in the road where the solid rock gapes open and its shadow drops away and as some of the coolness is lost we are dazzled by the sun's last rays and my mother lowers the sunshield above her and we see one eye appear in the mirror which she turns around so as to keep an eye on us rather than look at herself; we are no longer hungry or thirsty, our warmish bodies ache pleasantly with tiredness. This is the crucial moment when we cross the legendary Babaou pass, with its dangerously steep slope whose bends are studded with crosses, a road that must have been fatal for many families; my eyes are glued to the window to get a look at this precipice that swallowed them up, and at this moment I yearn intensely for us to fall and in all seriousness implore my father: 'Throw us into the ravine! Throw us into the ravine!' Down on the other side of the pass is the sea, but I'd rather never have set eyes on it. There is nothing in the world I long for more than this ravine and I know that this longing is closely connected with the love I have for my father.

For my mother the nicest time is when she's in the restaurant just after the fuss of ordering and before they bring the iced rosé wine she likes so much, and she has her offspring in front of her, checking they are clean, smoothing a lock of hair, then lost in thought for a moment she sets her elbows on either side of her plate and rests her chin on her hands; she feels a great surge of pride, she is happy, her whole life is summed up forever in this moment.

In July we go to Aiguebelle, to a hotel for civil servants which is all pink. The brick-coloured floor tiles are cool underfoot and I love to slide my bare feet along them as far as the balcony when I come back from the beach in the evening and I'm a little bit sunburned, and my skin smells of salt and suntan lotion and the scorching heat has cooled down. I have few memories of this place: the arches of my feet touching the floor, the dazzling trans-parency of the sea, the first sensation of weightlessness

I get with my inflatable ring in the water and which makes me feel like a ballerina flying high above the stage the way they do in illustrated strips, and a dingy shed on the way back from the beach when the sun's at its hottest – just a garage that the hotel owners have turned into a bookshop for the holiday period; there's a huge pile of *Bibi Fricotin* comics that smell of printer's ink and adventure and which I rifle through day in and day out. When I first discover this treasure trove my father generously buys me two – I know why, he wants me to leave him in peace when he has his nap or whatever he does then. It's at Aiguebelle too that my mother gets a small skin discoloration, either with some cheap eau de Cologne splashed on a sunburn or which saturated the skin just before it; it's on her chest, high up. As time goes by it turns into a port wine stain that she tries to hide with one-piece bathing suits.

We spend August at Croix-de-Vie on the Atlantic coast in the Hôtel de la Plage, another in the chain of hotels for civil servants; it's on the seafront, in charming shades of blue and white, colours which sometimes even flood into one of the manageress's eyes, Madame Fortini, who is plied with doughnuts by her husband, the cook. My father settles us in then returns to Paris to work, sometimes coming back to visit us for the weekend. Left alone with us, though in a small, reliable family hotel,

my mother arms herself against the likelihood of attack.
In the evening after triple-locking the door and
checking that the key is in the lock in such a position that
it can't be dislodged by a key from the outside, on the
bedside table next to her, right by the light switch, she
sets her extra-large-size can of Elnett hair lacquer; with
its spray – regularly rehearsed – she will blind any horrid
man who does manage to push down the key. Once a
week she takes us to a pâtisserie in a little alley in the
village where there can only be five pieces of cake at
most – or just three – spaced out as a window display;
similarly lined up on a glass shelf is a row of monster
chocolates and my mother stocks up on these, selecting
the ones she wants at her leisure: a lavish dozen to be put
in a paper bag. For my sister and me this is a quite
unaccustomed extravagance. When we get back to the
hotel we take pleasure in recreating the pâtisserie's
layout on one of the shelves of the wardrobes, and
whenever we open the door what delight to get a whiff
of this chocolate, ever diminishing, mouthful by
mouthful. This is allowed at a particular time of day,
probably when we're at our most irritable. Lunch and
dinner are in the communal dining room where we
have our table and my mother has her bottle of rosé.
One day when the weather's bad and only one of the
guests is not at table, we are eating winkles and suddenly
we hear the siren sputtering on quietly, its sporadic

hoots now signalling a drowning. It is our absent guest who has drowned, and the taste of the winkles in our mouths acquires a faint flavour of his limp blue corpse. People often drown when it's high tide and stormy, and with the red flag hoisted. We nearly saw one of them one day, but he was far out, wreathed in wild foam, and our mother clutched at us so as we wouldn't run in. At each high tide we go to the Trou du Diable to see the geyser, mostly to wait, for sometimes it doesn't rise. It's just outside the village, near where the Coutuis live – those poor fisherfolk who are fortunate to be clad in our cast-offs – it's a rock crevice that acts like a cauldron on days when there's very high pressure, causing the water to boil up and burst into a spray. It makes a dreadful noise, like the moans of a giant or a captive spirit. There are stories that during the war the Trou du Diable was used to help fugitives and people from the Resistance escape; a tunnel was dug out connecting this well and the cellars of the big mysterious building across the road, which we will soon explore.

My parents give me a membership to the Pirate Club. My sister is really good at the rings and trapeze for the older ones; I limit myself to the seesaw and the little chute – there are two of them, a wooden one where the backs of your thighs tend to get scratched and a dark brown linoleum one that sticks to your bum and makes it smart if you don't put the smelly little blanket mat underneath you. Sometimes I go right to the top of the big one, but it's so scary from up there that I go back down by the rungs or scream for someone to come and save me. We go on the cable-way too; it's not as high as the big chute but the lever is so hard to hang on to and it stretches your arm, it would be perfect for knocking somebody out; latching it on the cable wire and throwing yourself into the void, and it makes your jersey ride up and show your bellybutton. There's a grown-up who stops us when we get to the end. I've got my Pirate Club badge; it entitles me to use the play equipment, and the gym contraptions, which I can't be bothered with, and the beach competitions, which I love, and the knives. It's old Madame Gravey, the head gym teacher's mother, who keeps them all locked up in her iron box. I can no longer remember exactly how you play: you impress your hand in the sand and push the point of the knife into the sand with your palm, and there's more to it than that, for then it's your elbow you have to stick the knife in with, and if you go on winning your whole body has to twist around the knife: with knife pricks pushed in from your cheek, your forehead, the top of your head. It's a very dangerous game if you play by the rules. On the day of the beach competition we buy *Le Figaro* to cut out the coupon for it, and we fill buckets with seaweed and shells to decorate the sandcastles. I always win a consolation prize: a paper bag containing stale caramels and some ragged Tintin cut-outs. The sand is very hot underfoot and I'm playing with the great big blue ball that belongs to the Club: this great mass of rubber is called Nivéa and it has a handle you can sit on to make it bounce; my balance is never very steady. I am in my swimming trunks, bare-chested, sitting on the ball. Just then a boy comes by and he tells me that I am not like him; I hadn't noticed before. I have a hollow in my chest while other boys have flat chests or ones a bit swollen. I don't remember the boy's exact words any more, but they cut my life in two.

Whenever there's a very high tide we wait for the sea to go right out, then, before the tide comes in again, we get busy hunting for crabs. We put on white rubber espadrilles so we don't slip on the seaweed and with a bucket of seawater in one hand and the net in the other we follow the shore right out to the big weirdly-shaped rock that's at the entrance to the bay; sometimes you can see it as a bear, sometimes as a man with a child on his shoulders. The most exquisite thing about days like this is when you dip into a pool and out come a whole cluster of shrimps and your fingers must be deft and quicker than those translucent bodies, playing dead and writhing and slipping through the meshes of the net.

My father lies to me; he tells me that he had that hollow in his chest too, but it filled in as he got older, particularly with exercise. There are different versions: my mother says that my sister and I both have it because of wartime deprivation, an incapacity to absorb calcium. We need to sunbathe, swim a lot, do the backstroke and keep up gymnastics. It's 'remedial' – how hateful words can be. 'Hygiene' spoils all the pleasure I could have derived from having a father who's a vet, just like that. And the fact that gymnastics are remedial demoralizes and disheartens me. I'm taken to remedial gymnastic teachers who push me around and walk all over me and tire me out in the futile attempt to remodel this puny frame of mine. To measure the lack of progress I go to the hospital for a free consultation and in front of all the interns the cavity is filled with a tiny amount of water out of a syringe marked in millimetres; when I raise my chin there's a horrid little triangular puddle. At one point there's talk of an operation: the sternum is split vertically, the most concave section of the bone is cut away from the pericardium and turned around in a procedure that makes a ligature with the ribs. There are risks: it might end up sticking out or this structure might collapse. My parents decide against it. My heart and respiratory functions have been measured and appear to be fine, I've got all my seawater swimming diplomas, from twenty to five hundred metres.

It's lovely coming back to the flat after the holidays; it has a smell, it smells of our family and it's such a reassuring odour, the smell only intensified like that once a year, with the windows shut and enough time for cooking smells to evaporate completely so that all that remains is a very pungent mixture of furniture wood and varnish, a faintly mouldy smell from the curtains and bedcovers and the merest whiff of it from the paint on the walls. I dash into my room to check that everything's there; I take possession again. I open a drawer where there's an even more concentrated bit of that smell, I take out my stamp album. At this moment this is what I'm happiest of all to rediscover. It is a big flat volume, bound and covered with fancy coloured paper; I turn the pages very gently so as not to disturb the stamps and for the pleasurable rustling of the fine tissue sheets and the transparent strips underneath them. I collect German stamps. On them are the faces of scientists and their fantastic inventions that make you think about astrology and prehistory. But better still there are the colours whose names in the catalogue make them even more luscious. I buy the new edition every year and it is desire for the colours that sends me into ecstasies more than anything, for they are always sepia or indigo, and the picture is of secondary interest.

★

I've no idea where this eroticization of Germany comes from; I bought a road map of the country, heaven knows it's ugly, coloured in pale, all creased with folding, and yet I feel drawn to this vast shape that's slightly flared in the middle as I might be drawn to a body. The names of the cities and how I imagine arriving in them have the intoxication of erotic daydreams: Sigmaringen, Leipzig, Hanover, Bremen become more desirable than women's breasts.

On my father's uncle's typewriter, the same one I'm still wearing down my index fingernail on, I concoct a newspaper; extracts feature prominently; from my picturebooks and schoolbooks I select the passages I like best and copy them out with some notion of making them fit together. The preparation of the newspaper, secret throughout, lasts several weeks. When at last the newspaper is ready and stapled together I present it to my father who then buys the master copy at an exorbitant price, as he does the two carbon copies, so as to stop me from going to sell them in the street.

My mother isn't religious, she's superstitious about little strokes of good luck or avoiding bad luck; she plays patience and does crosswords, she asks the cards for good fortune and happy marriages for her children and the crosswords are to keep her wits about her. She reads

Jours de France, Ici Paris and sometimes *France Dimanche*
too; in one of these trashy papers she sees an advertise-
ment for a little magnetic cross mounted on imitation
gold, the Vitafor cross. She sends away for it in the post
and it arrives shortly, a shoddy little square cross, tacky
magic in the guise of bogus jewellery; she applies it to
her skin on that port wine stain that nothing can get rid
of. Some years later, having acknowledged the futility
of this conjunction, instead of throwing the cross
angrily into the river she will put it back in the box it
arrived in at the bottom of some drawer. Every time she
notices the advertising for a new competition she buys
the newspaper running it and for a few weeks devotes
herself completely to researching material in order to
win. She fantasizes about it aloud; if it's a trip to
somewhere far away she starts looking it up in the atlas;
if it's a large sum of money she starts dividing it up and
spending it. She buys furniture. But she never wins,
only a few teabags once, and after cutting the coupons
off packets of breakfast cereal she gets back a pathetic
book of discount stamps. One summer I'm on my own
with her in Toulon and in the scorching heat she drags
me off to the municipal library in search of information
about Napoleon; she's got nearly all the answers to the
questions in a new competition, there are just one or
two she's short of and she pesters a librarian to set her on
the right track. Dashing after her behind the man in his

grey overall through those hushed rooms I feel perhaps a little bit ashamed. I know she has already lost.

Twice a day passing a bookshop window on the number 21 bus, I keep falling in love from afar – two thicknesses of glass away – with the same tiny image. The cover of a book about Bonaparte which shows him on a rearing white horse, his hair and clothes flying in the wind, his hand outstretched towards the battle. I picture myself beside this image, owning it. One day when I'm not at school I get off the bus with my father and we walk to the bookshop. But the picturebook costs too much. Shortly it disappears from the window. To make up for it my father takes me to the Invalides, to Malmaison. I collect all the postcards of Bonaparte's portraits. The one I like most of all is the one Gros painted of him on the bridge at Arcola: a youthful Napoleon holding aloft a standard that envelops him and whirls about him like a cloak. I still hesitate to kiss it.

One evening as we are going past les Halles my father takes me to his office to collect something he'd forgotten. Slaughtering is over for the day, the whole place is silent and empty, the only thing I notice is the darkness of an alcove that must be my father's office. A few years later les Halles are demolished and the slaughterhouses moved to la Villette. One morning, contrary to custom, my father wakes me while my mother and sister are still asleep, and takes me with him. It is a filthy winter morning with day breaking over a featureless stretch of grey ground; we're walking on large cobblestones and suddenly I become aware there's blood flowing in the gutter, an approaching sound of wheels, blindfolded animals pulled along with rope; my father takes hold of a steel valve and gives me a demonstration of how they're killed, the pistol held to the head; 'They don't cut their throats any more, the way the Jews do,' he said. At once I feel the cold valve on my brow and the spiked steel bar pierces my skull. There will be mornings when I wake up at the time when they kill the animals, unhappily alert to their death throes.

There's pus coming out of my little willy; sometimes I can't shake it off, even if I pull on the skin every time I pee, before and after as I've been shown. It won't come out, it hurts, and the skin fold often turns septic. I'm taken to the doctor, there's talk of circumcision but my parents are against it, my mother particularly so it seems, for isn't Uncle Georges circumcised? Didn't it create problems for him during the war? It wouldn't do if there was another war . . . I think I heard my mother say she prefers men who aren't circumcised. It's my father who takes charge of my willy, always at the same time: after I've finished my homework and before dinner; for this delicate operation the two of us lock ourselves in the bathroom. I don't like it, it stings. He has boiled the rubber douche bag and after checking the temperature of the water he dilutes in it an acid liquid, Dermolactyl; I'm standing up, he's sitting on the edge of the bathtub. I've got nothing on my bottom and I've got to hold a plastic tub under my willy for the polluted water to drain into, and my father holds it with two fingers and gently slides the nozzle of the douche into the hole through the skin, after testing the temperature once again with a little spray on the back of his hand; he presses the douche bag and we see the water in the bucket coming out a kind of yellow with little threads in it, and sometimes eyes like when you boil water. My father has seen and touched my willy so many many times that I ask to see his. He baulks at this. I insist. He submits. I'm staring at his trousers as he opens his flies and that's when I see something I've never seen again in all my life: a kind of threshing ringed beast, cork-screwed and blood-filled and raw, a pink sausage ending in a cone-shaped knob. At this moment I see my father's prick as if it were skinless, as if my eyes had the power to see right through the flesh. I see something anatomically separate. It's as if I see a superimposed and scaled-down version of the shiny cosh that he brought back from the slaughterhouse and puzzlingly places on his bedside table.

My father has the knack of using particular products or brands whose names have assumed a very special significance for him: he shares his Vademecum mouth-wash with the Queen of Denmark and her entire court; for foot hygiene the only product good enough is Mycodécyl powder; the only aftershave the antiquated but peerless Hyalin block stamped with the slogan 'Darling how soft your skin is tonight!'; the only eye lotion Chibroboraline and Optrex drops with their little eyebath; and the only poultice Rigollot. He likes their labels. He's the same when it comes to his hats, even though he's not one for stylish dressing. A good hat is a Motsch hat, bought on avenue George-V, with his monogram picked out on the leather of the lining; the FG which he so much likes to show me.

Except in photographs and from the silky feel of a lock of baby curls, an infant sacrifice, I've never known my father's hair, but I would like to. I preserve chestnuts in jamjars filled with alcohol and I also macerate a few rose petals. I mix them with thinned down poster paint and mashed banana, which I then rub vigorously on my father's bald pate; he is good enough to co-operate with this hopeful enterprise.

There are rules for looking after children; when they have stomach-ache they're given Biolactyl out of a bottle and Ganidan tablets. When they have a cold you rub Vicks Vapour Rub under their nostrils, on the bridge of the nose between the eyebrows and a touch on the chest. When it's a chest cold they get a mustard poultice that they are covered in right down to the hips under their pyjamas, with a towel in between so as not to get everything wet. It's ice cold, then it gets hot, then it burns, then it becomes so unbearable you can't even look at the pictures in your album, they pile on the agony; you scream, but you must be brave enough not to, you have to be manly, think about the holidays, then the relief will be lovely when it's over. The fiendish wrapping comes away from the skin with a strong smell of mustard. The mother's fingertip touch, simultaneously dreadful and caressing, seems to peel away the scorched skin with it; the very lightly patted puffs of talcum are sweetness itself on the verge of a swoon.

I've seen my father apply cupping glasses to himself. He's known in the family for his bravery; he cut out his own tonsils one day with a pocket mirror held to his wide open mouth. When the tow rope of his beloved boat, paid for with money cadged from his mother, falls on his finger and crushes it, he picks up the pulp and shapes the flesh back into the form of a finger.

The beloved boat is a four-berth sailing boat, six and a half metres long with a plastic hull, a Golif called the *Doher*, the first syllables of my sister's and my first names. It's the first day of the holidays, we're taking it down to the South, where we're all to spend the month of July together. We leave the Ezanville house where the boat was in storage and we take the main road through the forest of Fontainebleau. It is a fine late afternoon. For once the worst of the traffic is over. Suddenly, as we're on an endless downhill slope, behind us the boat begins to career from one side of the road to the other, until it winds up dragging the car with it. The tow coupling has broken. Nervously my mother asks my father what's happening and, as he tries to straighten the wheel from left and right, he answers in a pitiful voice: 'There's nothing I can do, nothing I can do.' We come to with our hands on the broken glass and our mother telling us not to cut ourselves. Some people take pity on us and pull us out of the car one by one. My sister is in fits of laughter. My father's white sailing boat is lying on the verge with the hull split open. It's the first time I see him cry.

My father leaves the slaughterhouse, he does dairy inspections. There are different working hours, he has a driver and he is given a pistol. I know he hides it at the top of his wardrobe in the hallway. This wardrobe is his lair and we're not allowed to open it. You would have to climb up on a stool to find the revolver but its presence in this cupboard has a way of permeating the whole apartment. My father brings home a microscope and shows me microbes. So it's all because of these filthy things that we have to wash our hands ten times a day, never stick our fingers up our bottoms, never suck them, and never touch old books, for they carry diseases.

My sister has set fire to her room reading at night with a pocket torch under her duvet so that my father wouldn't see any light under the door. But she put it out by herself, beating the bedding against the wall and opening the window to let the smoke out. When my mother goes into her room in the morning she finds it in ashes. My parents no longer have it in them to thrash my sister, she stands up to their blows with too much dignity.

It's not Bonaparte I love, it's Georges Guétary. His are lips I can go so far as to kiss on the record sleeve of *Monsieur Carnaval*, his new operetta. I go with my father to the record shop on boulevard des Italiens to make sure there isn't a new record out or an old one I might have missed. When I find out he's going to be on television one Sunday afternoon I turn up with my parents at the studio door in a corridor at the French Broadcasting Centre. I wait along with a few foolish, lovelorn old women, the only little boy there. Georges Guétary appears, half made up, with his wife and his costume bag and I go up to him to make my great declaration of love. He takes hardly any notice, carelessly signing the photo I hold out to him. There and then he loses one of the last buyers of his records.

On Sunday mornings my sister and I are made to go to mass, otherwise we don't get the ten francs weekly pocket money that means we can go to the cinema in the afternoon. Mass is torture, I hate my father on Sundays. On Thursday afternoons I love him, he becomes my best friend. After lunch we go down into the street together, my mother watching us from the window, and right away I put my right hand in my father's left hand and he tucks them both into his pocket. We start to walk down rue de l'Amiral-Mouchez towards the number 21 stop, then we come to a halt and go back toward the number 67 stop. My father is resolutely indecisive. Are we going to the cinema or to the Palais de la Découverte? Are we only going to go to the Montsouris park to see the Punch and Judy show? Are we going to the Grévin museum? Or to the Molitor ice rink, but then we have to go back up for the skates? But what if we went for a boat ride in the bois de Boulogne, no, it's too cold, the lake will be frozen? Or if we were to go to the Vincennes zoo? Or to see the crocodiles at the Porte Dorée tropical aquarium? Or the Jardin des Plantes maybe, it would be nearer? But aren't the zoological gardens more unusual, more fun? Sometimes with this search for what we could do we just keep on going up and down the street under the amused eye of my mother – who maybe holds us magnetized from her window – letting the buses go by and in the end there's no time left to do anything and we just go for a little walk around the park and the hands in the pocket have had time to get nicely warmed up and are virtually sweating from the heat.

My parents love Louis de Funès and take me to see all his films: *Oscar*, *Pouic-Pouic*, *Hibernatus* . . . My mother gleefully enjoys making a comparison between my father's appearance and that of Louis de Funès. One Sunday, either because we're late for the start of the film or because the hall is full, we have to make do with some other film. We're at the Mistral on the avenue Général-Leclerc; there should be two other films on in the adjoining auditoria. Since the third one is ruled out altogether, the only choice left is *Histoires extraordinaires*, a film in different episodes with Brigitte Bardot and Alain Delon. It is banned to under-thirteens. My father is doubtful – I am only twelve and a half – and he checks with the man taking the tickets, who is not averse to letting four people take their seats in an empty auditorium. My father knows that I've read Poe, and it's one more reason for giving way. I watch this film with an interest and excitement that are quite new to me; it is nothing like any of the other films I've seen, not like *Big Feet Bertha*, with Jerry Lewis, nor *Sinbad the Sailor* which scared and delighted me, nor *The Black Tulip* with the dazzling Alain Delon in it, nor *Lawrence of Arabia* which terrified me so much that I begged my father to take me out. In the first episode, filmed by Vadim, you see a man and woman in medieval costume flirting on animal skins. In the second one, filmed by Malle, you see a barefoot little boy dangling from a winch above a cask swarming with rats. Then the third sketch comes on, shot by Fellini, and titled *Toby Dammit*. This character, Toby Dammit, is an English actor invited to Rome by the Vatican to star in a Catholic western. The priests producing it go to meet him at the airport; he is wearing an almost ecclesiastical garment, which he will soon unbutton to reveal skintight mauve silk trousers puckered with sweat, and a frilled white shirtfront that is equally sweat-sodden, open loose over a wax-pale torso. His colourless blonde hair is dirty and dishevelled. His skin is a powdery yellow and a mass of shadows shape a spider on his brows. His eyes are a washed-out blue. He is on an escalator, staggering about drugged to

the eyeballs, and he has a hallucination: a little blonde
girl with a sly smile who's pursuing him everywhere,
bouncing a ball that's too light. There and then I am
smitten, physically, by this character, dissolute and
repulsive though he is. As a fee the Vatican gives him a
brand new Alfa Romeo during a party which he walks
out of, belching. He tears through the suburbs of Rome
in the car and the whole film consists of this wild drive
through the night. He flouts the sign barring the way to
an unfinished bridge and soon it is his severed head that
the little girl is bouncing on the cobblestones. I come out
of this film intoxicated and bewildered as if I've been
contaminated by this new kind of cinema, (I shall
abandon Louis de Funès to scour Fellini entire, taking
me on to Buñuel then to Polanski), and madly in love.
The English actor is called Terence Stamp and I don't
know by what marvels of perseverance I manage to get
his address in London; he lives in a building called The
Albany, a name I dream about; I write him long long
letters. At night, while I'm waiting for him to reply, in
bed I press myself against the wall to make room for him
and we lie awake whispering under the sheets, kissing
and caressing one another. These are the loveliest nights
of love I have ever spent, and at the same time they hurt.
By day I drag my father around on a crazy quest; we
worm our way into the offices of the film distributors,
Marceau-Cocinor, to beg for the photos we didn't.

manage to get out of any of the cinema managers. The film isn't on anywhere, it's been a flop and I can't see it again. In vain I scour the record shops for the film music so that I can bring it all back, and I put a small ad in my favourite magazine, *Le Fantôme*. I put the two magic photos under the glass of my desk top and fog them with my breath, waiting for his body to rise out of this mist. Once my father, maybe finding me at it, asks in a voice that is steady but fierce with jealousy: 'What do you see in this guy?' Nonetheless Terence Stamp's new film, *Theorem*, is coming out and my father accommodates my lust; the film is for over-eighteens and, after hiding me under his raincoat, he tries to bribe an usherette, but we get thrown out of the cinema. I have to make do with the film poster tacked above my bed.

I get home from school earlier than expected; one of the teachers is away. My mother is always in for when we get home. I knock on the door as usual and no one answers. I don't worry for long, my concern rapidly turns into unease, a perplexing suspicion. My knocking has been heard and in its wake comes not the opening of the door, but a muffled sound of commotion, of furniture being stealthily shifted. It takes a while; things having to be put back as they were or whatever. I don't know; I don't know how to make sense of these indistinct sounds but I feel at once that I shall have to make sense of them and that doing so will lead me to some crucial discovery. Words pass between us as my mother tells me to wait a bit longer. The safety chain is fastened; it's only fastened at night, to keep out thieves. The unaccustomed sound of the chain at this time of day seems to me to make the situation all the more serious. My father is there, standing about awkwardly in the living room which is also their bedroom and which I have to cross to get to mine. And indeed I cross this room, without faltering and with not a word, to put away my satchel; I notice that the orange-pink bedspread, whose folds I can trace with my finger whenever I happen to sit on it, is not disordered; but a frantic look my mother gives my father so as to draw his attention to something, before I've even noticed it, so that he cups it in his hand and hides it away in a box in the display cabinet, tells me I should make a point of soon investigating this object. I straight away go into the kitchen to have my afternoon snack. It's autumn, there are tangerines; I push back the kitchen door so as to peel the tangerine straight into the yellow rubbish bin, absentmindedly watching the peelings fall one by one into the bin, and suddenly on top of the rubbish I make out something shiny and deflated, utterly strange to me, which I pick up to look at. I start to rub the transparent membrane between my fingers as it slides against its sticky stuff, trying to figure out what it can be, not knowing and at the same time realizing – a tiny bit horrified, with the horror overlaying the satisfaction of detection – establishing a connection between the feeling I had and my parents' commotion. I let the condom fall back into the bin and wipe my fingers on the peelings and eat the tangerine.

Moments earlier my father was the person I loved most in the world. Within seconds, just the duration of this fingering, he becomes the most hateful of beings. I don't know whether he realizes why from now on I vehemently refuse to kiss him. Why, from this moment on, for no good reason, his cheek disgusts me; why I won't climb onto his feet and bury my head in his trousers; why I mockingly stop him from calling me 'his friend' as he wants to.

The head teacher, Madame Repel, an English teacher who moreover had given me very good marks in her subject, wrote in the general remarks box of my report: 'A devious child'. She's a young woman with very short raven black hair and jutting breasts that are always in tight clothes. I curse her. Ten years later I learn from my friend Thérèse, who has become her son's girlfriend, that she was decapitated in a road accident in what I work out as the summer after the offence.

★

A friend, the son of the deputy director of the Santé prison, takes me into his room, which has bars on the window and which overlooks a roof patrolled by guards. Under cover of the shadows, we throw peelings and screwed up paper pellets down on these armed men.

A man has strangled a child and writes letters to the police deriding them. I identify not with the child but with the man. When his ugly craven face is revealed it almost supplants the love I have for Terence Stamp's face. Found in a left luggage locker at the Gare de Lyon is a stinking suitcase filled with the arms and legs of a woman; the head, thrown in a dustbin, would have vanished into the grinding maw of a refuse cart. This is a young man who has murdered his benefactress. Murderers excite me.

This summer, we, my mother, father and I, are on the boat berthed in the port of Porquerolles. My sister is in Germany visiting her Gammertingen penfriend; every so often we go to collect the mail at the poste restante and sometimes we get a letter from my sister telling us about her uneventful and studious holiday. But at the end of the month when we're waiting on the platform at the Gare de l'Est to meet her train, she isn't there and my father goes back along the platform a little nervously and my mother and I hang about at the front and suddenly there's a little woman standing in front of us, wearing a short curly black wig (my sister has long straight blonde hair), and with a fox terrier on a leash (my father has always said: 'No animals in the house!') and a tall wan-faced bearded man hovering behind her; I see that her mouth is trembling. The first thing she says is: 'We'll need to make some fast decisions – I'm pregnant.' With a scream, my mother makes an unconvincing show of fainting on the platform. My father tramples on her, almost by way of taking things in hand; he grabs the leash, kicks the dog and threatens the bearded man: 'Monsieur,' he says, 'I shall prosecute you for corruption of a minor!' He takes hold of my sister's arm and pushes her in front of him. She's sixteen and has given her love to the first man who paid her any attention. She set up her scam by stealing the linen from the topmost cupboard so as to sell it at the fleamarket. With her penfriend as her accomplice she got a hotel room in a neighbouring town with her boyfriend and had the penfriend intercept the letters she got from my parents. When I follow my sister into her room I am proud of her. Right away Switzerland is suggested, but my sister calmly and energetically refuses to have an abortion. A few days later the fiancé is allowed to come to the apartment; it's either the heat or the excitement of it all that makes him pass out.

★

I had read all my books. On the revolving stand at the newsagent's in the square at Porquerolles there's a paperback of Sartre's *Le Mur*: a green fist whose skin is being torn on a bleeding wall; and I buy it somewhat at random. It's quite unlike the *Arsène Lupin* and *Rouleta-bille* books I've been reading until then, but all the same very readable. The last story is called 'Childhood of a Leader'; in it there's a description of two men in a flabby embrace after vomiting. There could be nothing more revolting; but this isn't the reason why I am electrified.

For some years my father has talked about settling outside Paris, by the seaside. He has applied for a post at the slaughterhouse in Toulon, where the boat is; he is turned down. There's a vacancy at La Rochelle. My mother doesn't want to leave Paris. My father asks me what I think and what I do think at that moment is really a bit fiendish: I'm fourteen and my parents are a hellish pain; here's the only way to get them off my back, for in three years' time I'll sit my *bac* and if my parents are settled in La Rochelle they'll stay there and I'll be seventeen and because of my studies I'll just have to leave them for there's no university in La Rochelle, so I'll be able to come back to Paris and I'll be on my own at last as I long to be. Craftily I egg my father on to covet this post in La Rochelle. And he gets it. My sister has left to set up house in the suburbs with her husband, and their son is born.

With his candle Julian set light to a bundle of bracken in the middle of the hut.

The Leper came near to warm himself. Squatting on his heels, he began trembling all over. His strength was flagging, his eyes had stopped shining, his sores were running, and in an almost inaudible voice he murmured: 'Your bed!'

Julian tenderly helped him to drag himself to it, even spreading the sail of his boat over him to cover him.

The Leper lay there groaning. His teeth showed at the corners of his mouth, his chest heaved as his dying breath came more and more quickly, and at every gasp his belly was sucked in as far as his backbone.

Then he closed his eyes.

'My bones are like ice. Come here beside me!'

And Julian, lifting the sail, lay down side by side with him on the dead leaves.

The Leper turned his head.

'Take off your clothes so that I may feel the warmth of your body!'

Julian stripped, and then, naked as on the day he was born, he lay down on the bed again. And against his thigh he felt the Leper's skin, colder than a snake and as rough as a file.

He spoke encouragingly to him, and the other gasped out in reply:

'Ah, I am dying! Come closer and warm me! No, not with your hands, with your whole body!'

Julian stretched himself out on top of him, mouth to mouth, breast to breast.

Then the Leper clasped him in his arms. And all at once his eyes took on the brightness of the stars, his hair spread out like the rays of the sun, and the breath of his nostrils had the sweetness of roses. A cloud of incense rose from the hearth and the waves outside began to sing.

Meanwhile an abundance of delight, a superhuman joy swept like a flood into Julian's soul as he lay there in a swoon. And the one whose arms still held him tight grew and grew, until his head and his feet touched the walls of the hut. The roof flew off, the heavens unfolded . . . At school we have to study Flaubert's *The Legend of Saint Julian Hospitator*.

I've seen the poster advertising *Le Crapouillot*, a magazine that promises to lift the lid on the world of homosexuality. I don't know how to go about buying it; it's quite expensive and what's more I wouldn't have the nerve to go up to a newsagent with this magazine in my hand. At the display shelves I slide it inside a large flat *Nouvelles Littéraires* and pay without any problem. I have to hide it twice: in my room then in the luggage I pack for my trip to England. It's the first time I travel alone. It feels as if I'm carrying a delightful bomb. When the coaches get to Seaford the names are called out for each French kid to be placed in a family. A man and woman of forty-five take me in their car to a gloomy big house where they drink tea in front of the television. It's Sunday. After leaving my suitcase, unopened, in my room, I go for a walk by the sea; there are swings and I go on one of the swings and have a very strange feeling of freedom. When I get back the house is empty; I go through the downstairs rooms, calling out, getting no answer, and in the kitchen I find a slice of ham on a plate which seems to be meant for me; I wait a bit longer before I eat it. There's a thunderstorm. When I put on the light in the bedroom I discover a huge spider in each of the four corners of the ceiling. I go back to the toilet, where I had noticed a wall broom. I manage to knock the first spider onto the ground then to crush it, the second one disappears behind the chest of drawers. I try to dislodge it and a host of beetles runs out right under my feet. I leaf through my magazine to get my spirits up again. Then, fully dressed, I wrap myself tightly in the sheets. The next morning I go back round the house calling out. Still nobody, nothing to eat. I go off to school. When I get back in the evening there's still nobody there, I half suspected as much. I wait until the morning. I tell the woman organizer, who comes and visits the empty house, makes a telephone call and gets insulted. The woman works in a factory in London and only comes to the house at weekends. I am moved to the very comfortable little house of a working-class family. I'm so afraid my magazine will be found that I throw it

in a dustbin. On the first evening I'm sitting in front of
the fire in the tiny living room. Squatting in front of the
mantelpiece is the little girl of the house, a tiny thing.
She gets up and comes and sticks a needle in my cheek.

We've already been once to look the place over, in
winter; my mother and father and I crossed the big
military square, and had lunch in the brasserie, to which
I shall never return; we walked alongside the lycée wall,
I raise myself up on tiptoe to look through the bars of a
window and all I saw was the empty expanse of a yard.
By the time I get back from England my parents have
already moved in and redecorated much of the
apartment. My father has brought his boat up by way of
the *canal des deux mers*. We live at number 25 rue Paul-
Garreau on the sixth floor of a large light-coloured
building called 'L'Amirauté', which overlooks the
parks; from the balcony above the trees we can see the
sea. All the rooms are spaced out along the same side of a
long corridor; only the living-room, right at the end,
has panoramic windows that form an angle. My room is
between the kitchen and my father's study; in it is my
child-size bed with its blue-brocaded fitted cover above
which I've pinned Dali's *Crucifixion*, the light oak
wardrobe where my clothes and books are and opposite the window my desk with its three drawers
and its protective glass across the top; the photos or

reproductions I've slid under it haven't got too muddled up during the house move: photos of the dancer Jorge Donn, Dali's *Tuna Fishers*, my photos of Terence Stamp. A blind closes off the glass door which my parents can go past at any time by way of the balcony. But I've got a new routine, one that has taken downright nerve: I close the door of my room as soon as I'm inside. It is the beginning of September, a few days before school goes back, when I arrive in La Rochelle. My father, who wants me to be a doctor, has made me take a maths class. But there's only one thing I'm interested in: acting. I did some at the lycée Rodin with the company directed by a French teacher, Monsieur Naubreaux who, happening to see me in a corridor, cast me as the shepherd in *The Marriage of Figaro*; I have only a few lines to say but once I'm on stage I'm filled with such happiness that I'm beaming with smiles, then someone drew my attention to it and I stopped. I go straight away to the youth centre to find out about acting classes; but there's something not right, either the place, or the reception I get from the people I speak to, or else the times of the classes, and I know immediately that I won't go back, this won't be my stamping ground. I wander on around the town and pass by the municipal theatre in rue du Chef-de-Ville; I get some information about programmes and membership and as I'm leaving the theatre, on the left, in a glass box affixed to an ugly openwork grey door, I catch sight of a notice announcing the resumption of acting classes. I climb a darkened staircase, knock on a door, and real grown-ups answer and are extraordinarily nice to me. In no time I'm hearing that they just happen to need a young boy for the next play and as I go back down the staircase I'm so giddy at the thought that I might fit the bill that I practically fly over the steps. There's been little enough time to regret my decision not to enrol at the youth centre. The first class is one evening, in a place they call the studio, in an attic right at the top of the theatre; I notice there's a door directly off the staircase onto a balcony corridor and this endows the place with instant importance. The lights have been turned on, daylight is gradually fading, there's a group of young adults that I join in with and we are asked to faint, to laugh out loud, to shout, things that are very hard for me but which I force myself to do as if they were natural, since the difficulty of producing them is smaller than the fear of being conspicuous; screaming and falling about like the others is the best way of becoming a part of this group. It's a woman running the class, Marie-Claire Valène, the director of the resident company, the *Comédie de La Rochelle et du Centre Ouest*: a slight, nervous woman with straight short ash-grey hair, a somewhat thin mouth and a lovely clear-eyed way of looking at you. At the end of the class she allocates parts and suggests scenes to work on. A tall, fair-haired boy with a slender face has been wanting for a while to work on a scene from Camus' *Caligula*, but has no Scipio. And at that moment, with a strange smile which I notice simultaneously triggers some kind of emotional response in the group, she points to me and says I'm ideal for cueing Philippe. The next day I go and buy the book in paperback, which has a blood red cover with Gérard Philipe's face upon it. I immediately read the scene in question and the words, the phrases and the stage directions simultaneously electrify and terrify me; I'm going to have to be very close to this boy, he's going to touch my hair, he's going to speak into my mouth, he's going to press my head against his thighs, and I wonder how that will be possible without cutting things out. In the afternoon when I leave the lycée, where my status as a Parisian and this elevated and adult-connected new activity give me an unaccustomed poise, I go to the studio, which is bursting with sunlight and where Philippe is sitting on a chair waiting for me just as I had both hoped and feared, and I can feel his breath very close to mine and in no time he seizes hold of my hair and thrusts my face against his thighs, which are bathed in summer velvet, sand-coloured slenderness, and what I breathe in is suffocating. My days all strain towards nothing but this: the return to this text, these movements, this person. Philippe is at the same lycée as me, he is seventeen, he is in the top class and in the morning the first thing I do as I make way there hurriedly is to cross the three courtyards of the old convent so as to spy from a deliberately kept distance, amid the assembled group of grey-overalled boys smoking, a sight I can then carry with me all school day long: the head of hair that is tallest and blondest and which can only be his.

We have performed our scene; when we act it we are in a state of tension that I have never before experienced and whose pitch is an almost imperceptible quivering of each word and each gesture, yet drawing them up into a kind of electric arch that makes our breath vibrate and gives a nimbus of blonde light to his hair whenever I raise his head; the alternating ebb of his breath and mine has the smell of a young heart (I ought now to re-read those lines, for the first time, but these are emotions which I shall spare myself; strangely, there is something overwhelming about these very beautiful memories which I have taken so long to recall). This scene will reach a point of despairing emptiness and abandonment where we can no longer play it, nor go back to it nor perfect it, when we will be ordered to stop, as if to do otherwise were madness, and this order will seem to be the seal of our separation. A real love was conjured and given body in the scene whose words we can no longer speak again; separated from our characters, who were ourselves, we have had to invent our own lines. We rehearsed them and played them indefatigably, side by side, walking in those parks that surround my house, always with a small missing line that we stop ourselves from uttering, and even from expressing to ourselves, such is our uncertainty of it, such our too great certainty, such we pretend still to doubt it, and such we fear the cruelty of the other. We walk along the bank of a stream, and those words that are the loveliest on earth, that everyone utters or can utter, even if just once, melt into the murmur of the water. Our hands are close but the electricity attracting them has the opposite effect of keeping them apart in a torment that is happy. And at each bend, behind each copse, there is a shadow at our heels, which vanishes just as we could take it by surprise. And I know that this shadow is my father's.

I fall sick and he won't let me got out so long as I am convalescing. I still have a slight temperature. I sulk. I'm in the big living-room with my mother. I've just written a letter to Philippe and entrusted it to my father to take post haste and put it through his grandmother's letterbox in rue Gargoulleau. My father has become my love messenger, suffering in silence yet proud of his importance, he submits to this task; not once does he trespass upon the secret of the envelopes, he knows all too well what they contain. On his way back he brings me up the letter which has been left in our box, the nicest present he can give me, for when I'm sick he always brings a present. But he is still not back yet and in this big living-room, beside my mother intent on filling in a crossword puzzle, I am at a loose end; it's still a little early to go on with the letter I am endlessly writing and which I am sorry to have to break off so as to send it, and I take one of those sheets of paper and write a poem whose subject is the creation of the world. Then I write another one, then a third, but then I stop writing poems and start writing film sequences.

That's what I see and want to compose: camera movements. The camera picks its way around a village at dawn, bearing down on faces, the tones an ashy grey, colour lent by blood, its source a child. I write these synopses in my exercise book during the maths lesson. I've taken my seat alone at the back of the class; the teacher, Monsieur Gazeau, leaves me to it; at class tests I hand in blank sheets of paper. And always in the margins of the exercise book I draw a thin face, shaped like a knife blade, always the same. I think I have never seen it, but invented it.

I am summoned to the headmaster; the maths teacher won't give me any marks on my report, since I do nothing. The headmaster tells me not to worry about it, to go on just as I am, that it's idiotic of my father to make me do science studies and that at the end of the year he'll have me transferred into a literature class, and he adds: 'If it disgusts you so much to dissect frogs, then don't do it, refuse!' He does not caress my face or my hair but his words make me feel as if he does.

When I come out of school I always desert the group I'm with and rush to the theatre. I dive into the studio and if it's empty I go back down and slip into the theatre balcony through the door on the stairs. It's dark, the seats are a turquoise colour, I hide away in the back row, there are men at work on stage, sets being put up, actors or dancers rehearsing, sometimes they sense that I'm there and stop, shading their eyes from the spotlight and squinting into the darkness, calling me and I don't answer, taking off with a clatter of the seat or just sliding down into it. I'll go and see them in the evening, I'll be a member of the audience seemingly like any other, but I already know them. The woman at the box office gives me complimentary tickets on the sly. And under the glare of the lights the turquoise seats have a newer and more indifferent air about them. These seats are where everything happens for me. Philippe is sitting beside me in the orchestra stalls, my father behind us in the balcony.

One autumn afternoon we go to see *Woodstock*, and it is agony not to touch him, not to be able to admit that I want to touch him. I am afraid of him knocking against me. When we leave the cinema, out in the sun we slip away towards the park. We go on with the conversation of friends that endlessly stalks love. And then out of the blue I plunge right in, words I have said to myself a hundred times, but they're not the ones I come out with: 'I think I love you.' I'm trembling with fear, he can see and he clasps my hand. His silence at first has a ghastly resonance: he is groping for words. Gravely we tell each other that this love cannot be the same one that others denigrate. I imagine the first embrace as unforgettable, and that, having attained it, I'll no longer have a reason to live.

For New Year's Eve my parents let me go to Saint-Martin on the Ile de Ré, where I sometimes go riding. We're to stay overnight. My hopes are raised. In the evening, in the dining-room decked out as a ranch, we drink wine with the actors from the company and eat those fat flattish oysters whose flavour I shall always seek out. Late in the night the bedrooms are allocated. One of the women opposes my sharing a room with Philippe, but someone who is in the know mocks this prudish prohibition. I am at last alone with Philippe in a room that is unheated and has just one double bed. He half undresses and leaps into bed quickly. I am still standing there fully dressed. One of my legs is shaking helplessly. I turn out the light, hesitate, then one by one I take off all my clothes with the weight of a sacrifice, and walk up to the bed naked. I lift the sheet and hold out my hand, he reaches out a hand and checks that I am naked; annoyed, he sounds just like my father, the words so horribly disappointing: 'You're crazy, you'll catch a chill, hurry up and put on a sweater!'

We hold each other close all night with no thought of sleep, we embrace venturing neither to kiss nor feel each other's genitals, being so close is a joy so great no other is imaginable. But in the morning he turns over onto his belly and frustratedly rubs himself against the rough sheet, gives a little sigh and relaxes; I reach out underneath him, he tries to stop me and I recognize that cold jelly of my father's. I leave the bedroom to go to the toilet and the guy who took our side has left his finicky wife and is hanging around, maybe waiting for me; he sees me sniffling: 'So it's the waterworks!' he says avidly. I feel like smashing his skull. I leave the house, it opens onto a small embankment that dips down to a thin strip of sand, a few beached hulls, it's low tide, a bright soundless day, I sit down in the sun, someone goes by on a bicycle and it seems as if this man or woman is taking a good look at me so as to deliver my glorious message to the world, or maybe too he's unaware of me, and the bumpy sound of the bike fades in the distance and wide-eyed I ransom my soul to my surroundings. I have the certainty of an eternity, of being myself eternal.

It is only in the turquoise seats that we can touch one another again, lay our arms on the armrest to seek out a hand, brush against it, clasp it, caress it, and going further, catch at a sweater, feel that amazing texture of the skin. Philippe uncoils my penis from my trousers, warms it in his hand, pulling on it, rubbing it. In this way I see a whole season of Bergman films without seeing a thing. In the evening when I get home I find on the tip of my penis, now dried or glistening still, some drops of that nectar which takes so long to come.

Once after dinner I'm in a hurry to go out with my father to meet Philippe at the theatre where a woman singer is performing. To my annoyance my father is dawdling in the bathroom, always one to be cleaning his teeth and washing his bum at the drop of a hat. I'm afraid we're going to be late; it's as if my father, usually punctual, is being a slowcoach on purpose. I get impatient, open that bathroom door and make a caustic remark; he slaps me, I slap him back, he pushes me into the corridor and slaps me again, I slap him back again, my mother comes to the rescue begging us to stop, I open the outside door and go out into the corridor and call the lift, my father has his trousers on again, he rushes after me into the lift; I've pressed the ground floor button and the sliding doors have closed again, my father presses the sixth floor button and once we've gone down he tries physically to stop me from leaving the lift, grabbing hold of me; I push him away, the doors have closed again, I press ground floor again, then once we are back on the sixth floor the door opens and my father tries to make me get out. We go on fighting and soon we're at the theatre where Philippe and my father give one another a challenging look, like two rivals.

I get the feeling that Philippe is turning cruel. I can't understand why he's told me he has burned my letters. I would surrender his only over my dead body. He leaves with the company to go on a tour of Morocco, playing a small part in *Knock*. Waiting for three weeks without a letter is more than I can endure. I am desperately alone in my turquoise seat at the back of the balcony. I fear the worst: either he's dead or he no longer loves me. He comes back with a story about a love affair he's had with a young boy he met in Fez; it hadn't occurred to me that another love could get so close to ours and catch it unawares, I have no way of fighting back and no hatred; I suffer but don't yet recognize jealousy.

One rainy afternoon I'm waiting for him at the theatre cafeteria, getting restless; he arrives carrying a white book, opens it at a certain page and holds it out to me with a fingertip pointing at a line; I read: 'Suck my member hard, like you suck an ice cube.' These are poems by Genet. The words have struck home. Mockingly, Philippe closes the book.

Disappointed at not having been cast in the new production, he leaves La Rochelle to go and live with his mother, who runs a hotel at le Grau-du-Roi. I get his letters; nice, confiding, faithful letters. Time passes. He comes back. One summer we play Malcolm and Donalbain, the two brothers of the murdered king in *Macbeth*. Because I'm studying for my *bac* in French I have to be replaced for the first performances. Re-joining the company on tour, one night I walk into the make-up tent. He's there with the others, and out of the blue I hear him say something that cuts me to the quick and which at once becomes more memorable than all the most thrilling things we have experienced; he is complaining about my return, saying things were better without me, and I know he's having an affair with the boy who replaced me. We sleep together again, in a hotel at Noirmoutiers. Now that I know how to do it at last, I concentrate on jerking off his thin, slightly bony penis. He comes in my hand, insulting me because it's the only thing I know how to do. I still can't understand this nastiness. Yet, I get something out of it, unhappily caressing the extraordinary texture of his skin for the last time.

In six months I have grown up, I let my hair grow a bit and it's getting curly, I have pubic hair and by persevering I managed to make myself come, between noon and two o'clock, sitting on the toilet amid the smell of lavender paper, astounded by the simplicity of the action and the growing tickle in this slightly smelly tumescence which friction causes to fill the skin with blood then finally spit as it gives me an orgasm. Holding it back as long as possible becomes a science; I come for the second time in a sheet of paper that I number then mislay among other papers. I avoid coming in my bed, I'm scared of staining my sheets. In the morning when my mother comes into my room she throws back the bedclothes with a fearsome gesture as if she could read all my thoughts, as if she were an inspector of my dreams, and I sometimes feel shame when I give her a pair of underpants for the wash, for I know there's a stray yellow droplet on the cotton; she has a revolting way of deliberately undoing something that's been rolled up in a ball.

It doesn't take me long before I have a new lover: Jean-François, whom I met on a trip to Paris. I read in some newspaper or other that the Gay Revolutionary Front was having an open meeting one evening in the week in the lecture hall at Beaux-Arts. Anxious to go, I made a brief note of the announcement in the newspaper. And one evening during the All Saints holiday, or the February break, there I am sitting in that lecture hall in a crowd of boys shouting or listening, variously mournful or heated. A young man sitting right in front of me turns around and speaks to me; he has a faint blonde beard and he leaves the friend who was with him to take me to his place. There I encounter surroundings to which I am unaccustomed: a white-painted parquet floor, statues, a living-room converted into a photographic studio, and right away he photographs me in my scarf and Breton jersey. Then, I suppose, we must have kissed and jerked each other off, but I can't really remember. He doesn't fuck, he doesn't suck, and this suits me perfectly; I'll see him again. But I return to La Rochelle and he writes me a letter virtually every day, even two sometimes, and my parents begin to ask questions. I hide the letters behind some books right at the bottom of my wardrobe; occasionally I'd love to be able to tear them up as Philippe did, it would be convenient, but I don't like the idea. Whenever he can, Jean-François comes to see me at the weekend; he's an art director in an advertising agency, he seems to have plenty of cash. On Saturday, when I'm coming out of school, he is to be seen behind one of the arches in rue du Palais and I leave my classmate Sorin, who laughs saying it's just like me to go screwing this guy; Sorin has very soft skin, I love pulling his t-shirt out of his trousers to caress it. Jean-François takes a room in a hotel by the port. Some weekends he hires a moped like mine and we go to the Ile de Ré and Jean-François takes photographs of me on the beach and all over the place; he is happy and in love, I like him and it's nice to have found someone to jerk off with. We plan a trip to Rome at Easter and Jean-François arranges it from Paris, writing or telephoning to keep me in the picture. Shortly before we're due to leave I get sick and, in the wake of a few days of to-ing and fro-ing, my father summons my mother and myself to a solemn meeting in the living room. He tells me: 'Hervé, you can't go to Rome, I've had some enquiries made with the police about your friend Jean-François and there's something I have to tell your: he's a queer.' I take no more than the time to gulp, then tell him: 'Me too.' Then, with a cry of dismay, my mother makes another pretence at the bad fainting performance she'd tried out on the station platform for my sister's benefit: 'A daughter pregnant at sixteen and a queer son, what have I done to displease God?' My father, who's making visible efforts to keep his cool, tells me: 'Don't think I was taken in by your little jaunts to the Ile de Ré. You have to put that behind you now: it's probably harder to seduce than to let yourself be seduced, but it's time now you acted like a real man with some young girl.' He leaves the apartment. I'm left with my mother in a state of collapse, pitying her and despising her, and I tell her that I'm going to kill myself and I go off on my moped to the post office, where I ring Jean-François. I come back unabashed, with my mother begging me foolishly: 'So it was one of your jokes, did you just say that to annoy us?,' in a voice that makes it impossible to reply. From then on Jean-François loves me so stubbornly that the outcome is I stop loving him; he makes my life too complicated, I now have to lie so as to see him, hide myself away so as to write to him, pick up his letters at the theatre and his parcels at the main station, dismember them into different rubbish bins until all that's left is what will fit into my schoolbag and be concealed in my cupboard: books, records, flasks of perfume, little pictures he makes for me. And from now on whenever he comes to see me in La Rochelle, against my protestations, I live in terror that my father will discover us. One day my mother asks calmly: 'Doesn't your friend Jean-François write to you any more?' I reply: 'No.' Whereupon she turns into a madwoman, rummaging through the bottom of my wardrobe, and pulls out all the letters, shouting: 'And that? And that?' Shortly after that my father comes up with a really vile lie: at the slaughterhouse, where he's the supervisor, he got an anonymous phone call telling him that his son is a queer. He can't go on, with the threat of such a smear, even his job would be at risk and so maybe our livelihood . . . When I bend over your corpses, my dear progenitors, instead of kissing your skin I shall pinch it, and I'll pull out a tuft of their hair.

One evening early in August 1971, at Neheim-Hüsten, a mining town in the Ruhr, I go through the door of the riding school, where the sandy ground trodden by the horses is separated by a metal rail from the adjoining soft ground of a field. It is dusk. Were my shoes hurting? Does bad white wine become too good in plastic cups? I walk barefoot through the great clods of turned earth, feet shifting from the cracked ridge of the furrow to its soft dip, the driest of the powdery earth blotting up the mud little by little. The earth massages my feet, as if baptizing them; it is the purveyor of a new life, a life of the senses. I look up, the red sky enters my veins.

When I filled in the organizer's questionnaire, I made the mistake of noting that I ride. It was a man who met me off the train and at first I think he's my penfriend's father, but he's too young; he takes me off into a wood and there he gives me caresses. I shy away, we don't refer to it again and he introduces me to his wife; the younger children are already in bed and I'll sleep in the living-room. The man works for the one I'm to stay with, the manager of a cardboard factory, on his way back from an island in the Atlantic with his family. I'm woken up by a hooting car horn; the whole family piled into the car is framed on the other side of the window. When I see the man from the night before, the worker, I have the impression of having felt sickened by the sound of his animal groaning during the night; I won't see him again, the family collects me right away. I squeeze in at the back between the children: a little girl and two big blonde boys, Dietrich and Ludwig. Before even unloading the luggage we go and see the horses. They've been left alone for a month in this meadow and they're a bit crazy; the two boys seize hold of two manes and mount bareback and one of them lets me have his horse to do the same; I feel really embarrassed. Dietrich is my penfriend – the ideal boy: studious, good at school, good at the piano, good at riding; he tells me I stay too long under the shower and I'll go soft. Ludwig, a little younger, is the unruly one: he does nothing at school, won't play the piano, and he's mulish, only horses matter for him; two days later he's to go off to boarding school. I'm given his room. In the afternoon we go to the riding school. I'm with the two brothers in the basement changing-room, they are bare-chested in puffy pale blue underpants, they are magnificent, I feel as if I'm a traitor. The horses are being ridden again for the first time, they're nervous; an obstacle course has been set up in the enclosure around the riding school; the two brothers give me a demonstration; Ludwig persists in trying to reason with a horse that keeps on rearing up to unseat him and its neck bleeds from the whiplashes; Ludwig is covered in bruises; in the end there is nothing but a fused mass of furious writhing flesh bathed in sweat and streaked with blood, battling and clinging. That evening I find a pile of those pale blue underpants in the cupboard, I take one and jerk off in it.

Early in the morning the door of my room is opened; it's Ludwig, he wanted to pee, left his sister's room and eyes half-shut, without thinking went back to his own room; two hours later Ludwig will be nowhere to be found in the house. The two remaining children are forbidden by their mother to say a word to me; cigarette butts have been found in my room; while they were out I brought a girl back, something not done at my age. First of all a punishment has to be devised, an appropriate sentence; on a badly saddled ill-tempered horse I'm taken at a gallop into a forest littered with dead wood; I prefer to engineer my fall rather than be thrown, and I let myself fall off the horse, pretending to limp and ridiculing the ridicule. I go back to the forest with my French friends, Thérèse and Emmanuel, and we sabotage the course with treetrunks pushed onto the slopes; a systematic ferocity underlies this spree of ours; by a roadside Thérèse becomes the first girl to put her tongue in my mouth. Jean-François has sent me some grass in a parcel of books; with a sacrilegious prayer I raise my face towards the stained glass windows of Cologne cathedral and see the ghost of the colour blue spread between the ogival arches. In the house, where I'm left on my own now, I write while listening to Beethoven's symphonies. I write a story, 'The Blonde Prince'. Ludwig has come back for a weekend, I take him on an outing, it's raining, in the bus his thigh pressed against mine fills me with crazy heat, and on this gloomy bus ride a new little ribbon of eternity is threaded between his body and mine. When we get back to the house Ludwig takes me to the piano; we're alone, the rain is still dripping on the other side of the window, the rebel who practises on the sly plays the loveliest of pieces for me.

For the Easter holidays in 1972 my parents let me go on my own to Germany on a tour of the castles of Ludwig of Bavaria; my father, keeping tabs on me, must know that I'm no longer interested in travelling with Jean-François. In Munich I stay in a youth hostel; I sleep on the topmost bunk with my face against a nightlight, kept awake all night by drunks hiccoughing and stumbling about. The snowcapped domes of the cathedral are reminiscent of Siberia, I leave my luggage at the station and set myself down by a roadside with a plastic bag – book, notebooks, pencil, change of shirt, toothbrush. I'm heading deeper into the snow and I'm not dressed for it. A queer threw me out of his car on the motorway. At a snow-shrouded crossroads not far from a sanatorium that's still a touch yellow and pinkish under the frost I wait for a vehicle to materialize before my numbed senses. A madman comes by and carries me off at top speed towards the Brenner Pass. The snow melts, the blood begins to flow. In no time Venice spreads out before me, watery and fantastical, intoxicating, deliciously smelly and warm, as obsessive as the poison of some bliss.

I'm smitten by Marie-Jo, the company's leading lady. My schoolbag is full of steaks I steal for her at the Prisunic when I come out of school. Whenever I have the joy of eating dinner with her, if I have a pimple on my nose I'm capable of spending the whole meal with my face half covered by a scarf which I carefully detach so as to eat under it. One night in the country, Marie-Jo bends down to take me by the hand and makes me touch the warm jet of her urine against her lips. I'm reading Bataille at the time. We plan to go to country priests and make confessions of sodomy.

One Saturday in spring I run away; I say I'm going to school as usual and have in fact packed my briefcase as if I was, but on this fine morning I walk past the lycée and walk as far as the junction which takes you out of the town, and stand by the roadside and get taken to Paris. As soon as I'm there I go into a cinema in the Latin quarter where Jean Eustache's *The Mother and the Whore*, with Jean-Pierre Léaud, has been on for just three days. I have come to Paris only to see this film, I drink it in to the very last drop, I'm sated on it and adore it. When I come out I go and ring Jean-François' doorbell; he's out, I'm relieved, his concierge is happy to give me his key, I sleep in his orange bedroom where the shutters are always closed, and which is littered with the droppings of the white rabbit I made him buy, and in the morning I take off, leaving him a note asking him to record all the dialogue in the film and send it to me. On the red gloss paint of the lift in La Rochelle with the edge of a key I scratch these coupled nonsense words which have prompted one of the film's topics of conversation: 'soft and warm'.

Jean-François has knocked out an old woman who has a shop selling antique dolls behind the mosque. The shop is always empty, he went there one evening as it was closing with two suitcases. I love dolls with china heads, and they're a bit too expensive for Jean-François. Once the woman has been stunned by his blow, he fills the suitcases with the dolls and goes off home to sleep, dreaming of my delight. The telephone wakes him up with these words: 'Good morning sir, I am the lady you knocked out last night, your identity card must have fallen out of your pocket, in your haste I expect, it's the first thing I found when I came to, I've had my doctor certify the extent of my injuries and I'm waiting for you, bring back the dolls.' Jean-François explains to the old lady that he robbed her out of love. The lady thinks it would be good to win the friendship of so warm a man.

Jean-François encourages me to write, he wants us to do a book of children's stories together, and piecemeal I send him what I write, usually during French classes, and he sends me back photocopies of his drawings to illustrate them. He has shown a dummy of the book in progress to a publisher, who is interested. I am particularly keen that the book is completed before the end of the school year so that I can show it to my philosophy teacher, Monsieur Cejtlin, of whom I think highly. But my father, to whom I make the mistake of confiding about this project, dismisses it scornfully: 'Publishing a book is nothing, you only have to pay for it to be done', and he can make me a present of a book himself whenever I want.

In class I have a rival; his name is Olivier, he's bigger than me and I find it hateful to have to look up to give him my dirty looks; he has good features, a slight cast in one eye and nice wavy hair combed back. He is always top when I come second and goes down to second when I come top. We pretend to be unaware of this competition, trying never to let either our pique or our triumphs be apparent. We are so far above that: me with my theatrical activities, he with his literary activities, bringing out his poems in a little magazine from which I would be immediately excluded if I weren't too repelled to make the slightest approach to him, anyway they must be brilliant for he sent them off to a big Parisian writer, who wrote back, and he allowed a glimpse of the letter without handing it over to be read, despite my sneering impatience. We really hate one another and during a gym class – because we hate one another and because we hate gym – we stand opposite one another and touch one another up, each with a hand under the other's polo shirt. While his hand, climbing my torso, falls into the pit of its cavity, mine founders on the reef of a bone that protrudes like a ridge. Our eyes throw daggers when they realize we are the complement of one another, and that were we to fit close together the marriage of our hatreds would be perfect.

Philippe has gone to live in Paris, still in search of his father, supposedly a diamond merchant, whom he's never seen. I still act with the company: on tour over the summer I play a scullery boy in Goldoni's *La Locandiera*. I'm such a disaster at handling the sheets for the set changes that the director has decided to let me make a public spectacle of my clumsiness for the amusement of the audience. I'm smitten by the second scullery boy, Dominique. I take the least opportunity, in the dark, to throw myself on him and pull off his shirt; the first time, he takes my hand away in stupefied protest. 'You read too many books!' Indeed, with this first salary I buy myself a set of bookshelves.

I've ordered it, all in white wood, but I have to wait a few months before it's delivered. I'm planning to put it in the one-room flat I'll have in Paris. I've passed my *bac*, I'm studying for the entrance exam for IDHEC★, and I have to sort out a place to live. This is when my father puts up a desperate resistance: I am not to live alone in Paris, besides I'm still a minor, I'm to go and live with his mother in her house at Ezanville. He is very sad to have to give up this absurd idea. The success of my plan to leave home has been complete.

One last summer I go with my mother to the sailing boat moored at Porquerolles. The two of us are in this pokey space that has to be negotiated in a manner that's sometimes embarrassing; my mother has cystitis. We have the two parallel bunks closest to the cockpit, with a passageway between us that's scarcely the width of a body. One evening, as daylight lingers on, we are lying there side by side chatting desultorily before falling asleep. We are talking about this and that; I've drawn my knees up under the sheet and I'm jerking myself off

★Institut des Hautes Etudes Cinématographiques, the Paris film school (translator)

very slowly. I force myself to keep my voice level, its usual tenor unaltered. My mother keeps on talking and I keep on listening to her; there's nothing else at the back of my mind; my fingers get wet; this inadmissible memory still moves me.

Through the classifieds my parents find me a maid's room on the first floor of a new building, 54 rue des Entrepreneurs: a long narrow room with a wash-basin by the door and a barred window overlooking a warped and sooty rooftop. I set my new bookshelves on the left side of the room and the bed I've had as a child in the recess on the right. Some of my old posters find a new home on these walls. Jean-François, whom I see occasionally, gives me two potted trees that he's stolen from the entrance halls of buildings. I've failed to get into IDHEC, I don't know a soul in Paris, and in the evening I go and eat a shrimp salad at the Saint-Germain drugstore. A man asks if he can sit down opposite me and straight off asks me to go with him to Upper Volta in a plane that he flies himself: 'There's nothing complicated about going to Africa,' he tells me, 'you only have to take your Nivaquine every day for five days before you go; I've got some if you want it . . .' For a few days I keep in touch with this man by telephone without ever seeing him, planning this trip which we drop at the very last minute.

I've fallen sick, and since I have no friend to come and take care of me, after letting several days go by without any treatment, and with my temperature getting worse, I make up my mind to take the train to my parents' place. The five hours on the train have finished me off: when my parents come to the station to collect me I'm barely conscious. They put me to bed and call a doctor. But the doctor takes a while, and the totality of space begins to swing around me in my bed. I no longer have any stable vantage point for my body in relation to the scale of things around it: between the two there's a doom-laden disproportion, either the space is tiny and my body too huge to inhabit it, or my minuscule body is drowning inside the vast room. I'm afraid, I cry out. My mother comes to my bedside. I see her face leaning over me and what I glimpse in this face is an equation of salvation. I have to kiss her lips, urgently, or rather she has to kiss mine, this contact alone can return me to my rightful place in space, in the world, in life. If my mother won't kiss my lips all I can do is throw myself out of the window. I entreat her: my delirium frightens her, she goes away, I'm aware of her out in the corridor speaking of her fright to my father. I can't throw myself out of the window: my mother has closed it, even pulled down the blind. So I get up and go out into the corridor, my fists pressed against my eyes, stumbling against the wall in this enforced blindness, in this darkness traversed by flickerings and traps and shining monsters, getting as far as the bathroom, as far as the only mirror there is in this apartment; my mother refuses to kiss my lips, my last resort is the reassurance of my own face. I grope for the light, feel the cold wash-basin against my belly, and open my eyes in front of the mirror: I recognize myself and come back down to the level of sane men.

In Paris I have begun having intense sexual relationships which still leave me with a faint aftertaste of dirtiness, tepidity, vulgarity, bad taste, stupidity, disloyalty. And yet my hands feverishly caress bodies and my mouth begins to lose its disgust for cocks.

One fine spring weekend I come back to La Rochelle, my father has bought himself a camera, a small Rollei 35, he suggests I try it out, we put the film in the camera together, I want to photograph my mother, I get rid of all the fuss of her clothes and hairdo, wet her hair under the tap, have her put on a simple slip and tell my father to leave us alone. She's sitting in the light, I circle around her, and it's a moment of love and completeness that stops time as if we were waltzing together in some great ballroom flooded with brightness. When my father comes back we set ourselves up in the bathroom to develop the film; we're dumbfounded when we see that it's blank from end to end, that it hadn't caught properly in the camera. The light has gone, my mother has got dressed again and we know that in any case we can never replay this episode, that it has already assumed the helpless weight of regret. And that now this ghostly image strains towards something other than the image: towards narration.

After a year I leave the room in rue des Entrepreneurs. My mother has found a one-room flat to let in a block they've just finished building at 293, rue de Vaugirard, very near where my great-aunts live. I think it's September when I move, or June perhaps: it's a lovely day, at their insistence my parents did the moving and have gone to have a rest, and I'm left on my own in the flat that's been invaded by my mother's all-embracing words of advice about upkeep and her notes giving me detailed instructions about the water and electricity meters, about needing to defrost the fridge regularly, about the use of certain cleaning products. The sliding door of my window onto the balcony is wide open; I'm on the sixth floor and it becomes only too obvious that all my mother's notes, like arrows, merely point to this void where I should throw myself, to put a sarcastic end to their whole plan. I close the window and tear up the notes. My friend Bertrand comes by to see me, we drop some acid and start twirling round the empty, barely-furnished room to the waltz tempo of a sad old Bowie number, 'The Little Drummer Boy'.

I lost my watch a few months ago, that Lip watch from my first communion that I'm so fond of; I think the strap broke and it slipped off my wrist. Every now and then when my mother's in Paris on a visit she still comes to do my housework, she's got keys and we arrange it so that she does it while I'm out. One day when I get home I find set side by side on the table my watch and, upright, a little red and white plastic dildo that I'd long since forgotten about and which must have slipped down between the mattress and the wall. And all my mother did was write this little note: 'Darling rabbit, I'm delighted to have found your watch, I give you a kiss on the tip of your nose.' Now there at last is a charming story.

I spend a ghastly summer of '76 with my parents on Porquerolles; I am dreadfully in love with T. whom I met six months earlier and who, after a passionate three-month relationship, has decided affectionately but firmly to break it off. He writes to me now and then and the letters I write to him become so frequent and so tortured that all I can do is put them in an exercise book. In the evenings I end up having dinner sitting between my parents in a desolate tense silence; I have only T.'s name on my lips and I cannot know whether to speak it would be a defeat or a triumph. I hold it back, simultaneously cursing my parents for not making me spit out my confession.

A few months later I solemnly hand my parents an envelope 'To be opened only on my death'. Only too late do I realize that given their inquisitiveness and the anxieties they have about me they can't wait to open it and find out what's in it, even if it means gently steaming it open so as to leave no traces, for I haven't taken care to seal it properly. What is this pointless, cranky need to tell them that I disinherit them, I who own nothing?

The notebook with the love letters has become a book published by Régine Deforges: *La mort propagande*. I start writing another one immediately: *Il (Un récit de la mesquinerie)*. This is a series of texts where the I, in an everyday record of its thoughts and gestures, has a petty disguise in the identity of a fictional character. I never showed the book to a publisher in the end and it remains unpublished. One episode in it is titled 'The story of incest'. I am reproducing it here because it shows clearly the extent to which, seven years ago, I was prepared to devote myself to narrating the story of my parents:

If he wants to speak about the mother, she is a figure without consistency: she is effaced. Maybe it's the father

97

who has effaced her, or ageing, or motherhood. He lies to her absent-mindedly, inconsequentially, telling her offhandedly that she is pretty, or that her hair looks nice, although she can no longer believe him. He says: 'You aren't growing any older' while the truth is that he thinks: how she has aged. He can't stand her ageing, pretends to notice nothing, to be above it. He tries to separate her from the idea of mother, to see in her only a woman, but he cannot. She is not a self-possessed woman, she could never be called 'at ease with herself'. She has no arrogance. She minces about 'in company'. She has to have a little drink, wine soon makes her glow.

This woman is alone all day long, never leaving her house, once a week doing a large shop which she puts in the freezer. With increasing frequency she asks her husband to fetch the bread 'so she won't have to go out'. She says: 'I don't know what's wrong with me, I'm tired all the time.' In the apartment she talks to herself. She lies down. She sleeps. She says she often has migraines. When she's alone she doesn't watch television. She never takes a bath or a shower, claiming that her too-soft skin wouldn't tolerate water. But she rubs herself with eau de Cologne on a massage glove every morning. She went to her hairdresser carrying her copy of *Jours de France* to show her the photo, asking for a hairstyle like Michèle Morgan's. People have always said she looks like her – the eyes. When she gets home from the hairdresser she has a short-lived bout of flirtatiousness. She asks him: 'Do you think my hair's nice? Better than the last time?' Her hair is turning white but she won't have it dyed, not even a rinse. She says that it ruins the hair, that her husband wouldn't like it. With the touch of mascara she puts on around her eyes she might as well not be wearing any make-up at all. He doesn't like seeing her made up. He says: 'You look like a tart.' And what happens is that she tells people this: 'No, I don't wear make-up, it doesn't suit me, I instantly look like a whore,' and she laughs.

She waits for him. He hasn't even cheated on her. But he's never at home: he's at work, on the way to or from work, on his boat. He goes to the harbour every day. He sits in the cockpit of the boat, even in winter. He varnishes the doors, rinses out the sails, bails out water, sometimes he has it pulled up on shore and keeled over. It's a while since he's been out in it. He brings her back his wet pea-jacket, says there's been a storm. She makes him some chicken broth or a hot wine while she waits, says: 'I saw your sail out at sea from the balcony, it was too far for me to wave.' They make love once a week, on Saturday afternoon. He puts on a condom, flops down on her, comes quickly and immediately goes to the bathroom to wash. She is understanding: 'A man has his needs, it's normal.' Sticking a test tube into a side of beef, he breaks the glass in the meat and cuts himself on the finger; she takes care of it. An affection born of habit keeps them together. They regard despair as immoral. They never say: 'Things are going wrong'. Sometimes they argue, about trivia. Leaving for work each morning he tells her: 'Don't open your door.' Now he turns the key from the outside. He had never wanted her to have a job. She scrubs the bathroom wash-basin to a shine several times a day; in her house 'everything is spotless'. There are evenings when they sit side by side in front of the television and he holds her hand. She is keen on figure skating. Once the set is switched off after a play or a film what happens is that she starts telling him the story, repeating snatches of dialogue. She starts acting them out. It's always a moment of high drama that she re-enacts, like drunken tirades. He listens to her without making any comment, reluctant to say that he is irritated by this dramatic intrusion into their daily life. He thinks maybe she had too much to drink at dinner, he should have kept an eye on her. He tells her she knocks it back a bit, he 'keeps hold of her elbow' when she pours out plain old rosé wine. Sometimes he marks the bottle, or else he'll put his hand across her glass when she's pouring. She says she could have been an actress if it hadn't been for her legs. Sometimes she says she's wrecked her life, that she should never have met this man, that she's given too much to her children. She says she'd had offers to work in films when she was young, a producer, a customer in her aunts' pharmacy. If it hadn't been for these varicose veins she'd have gone places with those eyes of hers! She was in love with Pierre Blanchar, the actor in *La Symphonie Pastorale*. He loved Lise Gauty, the singer in *Chaland qui passe*. She says of her husband: 'I didn't love him to start with, then, in the course of time. . .' He enrolled in a Dale Carnegie course 'to learn how to speak in public and assert his personality'. Then the two of them joined a third age keep-fit club – for the elderly. She has bought herself thick black tights. She realizes that she's still supple. She does little rabbit hops. Once a month the club puts on a party, with a fancy buffet and a film show. They like that. They get friendly with other couples but turn down personal invitations, 'so as not to have to reciprocate', 'so as not to be under any obligation'. Then a newspaper ad makes him decide to lose weight by the Weight Watchers method. He buys some small scales and she has to weigh all his food before cooking it. He stops dieting because he notices that losing weight makes his face look almost skeletal, which is worrying. They put the little scales away at the back of the sideboard. They tell him they're afraid of Communism, afraid of not getting their pensions, afraid of being sent to camps for old people, afraid perhaps even of being separated from one another.

★

His father comes to Paris unexpectedly and one morning announces himself over the entryphone. He enters the apartment, trying to conceal his unease by feigning disinterest as he looks around, his eyes never lingering on anything. He must be thinking: don't disturb, don't be in the way. He looks so much as if that's what he's thinking that it does become annoying. But he doesn't hold it against him, he holds nothing against him any more. He finds him touching now. He'd forgotten that his father is so small, yes small – five feet six is small for a man. Out in the street his father says things like: 'I look like I'm up from the country, huh?', 'I've got no tie'. He doesn't quite understand why his father says that, what he means by it, what he's excusing. He tells his father to undo the top button of his shirt. His father is fifty-seven. He takes him to a restaurant where he goes regularly. His father tells him to decide and order for him, he doesn't even want to read the menu, he'll eat whatever *he* likes to eat. All the same he reads out the menu to him. He tells his father: 'You have a choice between egg mayonnaise, tomato salad and mackerel in white wine.' His father reiterates: 'I'll have what you're having.' He says: 'The waitress is pretty' and he doesn't mind his father saying that. And immediately he adds: 'It's my treat.' He would like to be able to have a spontaneous conversation with his father, but he can't, it isn't possible. All the same he makes an effort to tell him about his trip to England, but he realizes all he's been able to give him are the names of the towns he went through, a tourist itinerary. His father makes a stab at remembering, saying: 'I went there when I was sixteen.' His father asks him what he's writing at the moment. He makes an effort to answer, tells him about his play. His father had never read anything of his, except articles, and one short story, and he utters these words that both shock and impress him, while simultaneously giving him infinite pleasure: 'I can't but like what you write, it's the voice of my blood.'

His mother takes a delight, albeit a very weary one, in reminding him of those evenings when, after doing too much ironing, she had a migraine and he would make her stretch out on her bed, and would put out the light, dampen bath gloves with cold water and apply them to her forehead, changing them for fresh ones once they lost their coolness. With what sweetness he would perform these actions.

In the summer of 1977 I go back to Porquerolles for a few weeks to be with my parents one last time there. I write:

His impressions are unclear, they jostle against one another, muddled. Buried in parental benevolence, in mosquito nets and sweat and the salt that sticks to the sheets, he can concentrate on nothing. Total passivity takes over, ruling out even reading or writing. He is constantly eating the food his mother provides. Day and night he seems to be napping, without ever being fully awake or asleep. The way his parents have taken over his body anaesthetizes him. He lets himself drift into inertia. Abruptly he gives himself a tap on the head like a crazy man, to ask himself: 'What am I doing here? Why don't I get out?', then falls asleep again. Simple actions like eating, shitting, sleeping, take on acute significance, and fill up the time. Secretly his mother sniffs his body odours on his clothes. When he gives her some underpants or a vest to wash she says: 'It wasn't a luxury.' His father envelops his body in sundry attentions, building around him frameworks of net, bamboo and clothespegs so that he won't be troubled by insects while he sleeps. He massages his sprained ankle with gels and creams and bandages it. Or else he breaks little ampoules over it, whose liquid immediately penetrates the skin, leaving a residue of blue crystal. His mother tells him that she heard him moaning in the night, she came to look at him as he slept and spoke to him: 'You sleep with your body all twisted.' He can't bear to be faced with his nakedness in the mirrors of this rented room. Things get worse. He looks at himself naked in the mirror before he goes to bed and mentally photographs himself in different poses: face on, in profile, playing down or playing up his defects. He lets out his stomach, drops his shoulders, holds in his chest. And he says to himself: they are the ones who made this body. What can they do about this body though? Sometimes he held it against them that this was the body they gave him.

In a restaurant his father speaks these words to him that he has probably never said to his wife: 'You're looking wonderful tonight.' He also tells him: 'The main thing is that you are not suffering,' and it seems to him that these words sum up everything his father wants to say to him, everything he has ever wanted to say to him.

I am with my parents on the beach when I notice the arrival of a very beautiful young boy. Unaccompanied, he sets his towel down beside ours and goes into the water. I follow him with my eyes and after a long hesitation, tortured by the thought that it might be too late, I go into the water near where he is. He comes out and lies down in the sun without any fuss; I can see that my mother has noticed that my eyes are full of him. He has amazing green eyes, black hair, a lean muscled body. At one point he asks me the time and my mother frantically rummages in her bag to find her watch. He puts his t-shirt back on, flings his towel over his shoulder

and slowly disappears among the pine trees. As I watch
him slip away from me I'm in pain. From behind a tree,
just at the point where his vision is going to fade
completely, he turns and I can see clearly from this
distance of several hundred yards that his eyes are cast
towards me. My heart skips a beat, I'm on my feet in a
flash, asking my mother for the key to the apartment,
and leaving my bewildered parents, I get my bicycle
from where it's parked nearby and along the other, less
sandy path I reach the road where the boy is already
walking, and soon he's in front of me, his naked thighs
and legs, his towel still over his shoulder, back turned to
me and down from me, for the road slopes down, and I
brake, afraid of shooting past him like an idiot and not
being able to turn back, but there comes a point where
the steepness of the slope stops me from braking any
more without making myself conspicuous with the
funny screeching sound, and I shoot right past him
without turning round, and when I get to the bottom of
the slope I park my bicycle on the verge to wait for him.
I can see him now approaching me, at a pace that is
emphatically steady, and just as he is about to come
abreast of me I say hello and he answers with a smile and
I ask him if I can go along with him the rest of the way
and he says yes; we chat a bit, he tells me he's bored, that
he has no friends, he's at the Saint-Anne hotel with his
parents, and I suggest that he comes with me to my flat

to park the bicycle and then drink some orangeade before going out again for a walk; he wants me to wait for him while he goes and changes, then he's back looking even more magnificent, his thighs encased in tight white trousers that seem like some kind of wedding garment, and his smile more and more touching. Together we climb the staircase of the house where my parents customarily rent this little flat; first I take him into the kitchen, I open a bottle, we drink and I leave the two glasses on the table; we come out of the apartment again to go into my bedroom, which has a separate entrance on the landing; he sits on the window ledge, I'm sitting on my bed and I express my extremely intense desire to touch him. His refusal is full of sweetness and grace. I invite him to go and play a game of boules in the square and give him a choice between the two pairs of boules; he takes my father's. At the end of the game we part, after arranging a meeting for the evening, and I go back up to the apartment. My parents haven't returned yet, and I go to fetch the keys, which I must have put unthinkingly on the lintel of the staircase fanlight; they aren't there, I rummage in my pocket with annoyance, they aren't there either, and the locked apartment which is now impossible for me to enter turns into a space sealed off in the wake of a crime, pending a reconstruction. I go and sit down on the bed in my room, I hear my parents return from the beach, I announce to them my dismay at having lost the keys, saying it was probably in the square while I was playing boules. 'Playing boules?' my father asks in consternation, 'but who with? You don't know anybody here . . .' I tell him it was with a boy I met. Then my father says: 'This will all end with the police involved, or with syphilis!' We go to look for the keys, kicking away the sand on the alley where I've played, and we don't find them. Just when my father is telling me in annoyance that we'll have to go and fetch the duplicates from the owner, I find the keys in one of my pockets; my fingers had to have touched them, without being able to acknowledge it. We go back to the square with my father to play a game of boules. In the evening the three of us have dinner on the terrace of a restaurant in this same square. As dinner is ending the boy hovers round our table. 'How old is he?' my father asks. I say: 'Sixteen.' 'You see', says my mother. Then my father says: 'Boys are fine, but girls are even better.' I join the boy and we head into the darkness on the road to the lighthouse.

From 1979 on, my parents take up around a fifth of my journal. Here I'm going to reproduce the passages about them, filling in episodes that I missed at the time.

My mother, whom I've just seen, and whose face it was easier for me to take as it approaches a relaxed old age, no longer strained. Disfigurement, pure and simple.

My relationship with my parents has become reduced to routine attentions, fears, mutual anxieties. I am extremely cold with them, they no longer venture to ask me questions. But I think: just to let them see me, to see me still alive, is the greatest – the only – gift I can give them. Ceaselessly, silhouetted in the gloom of the kitchen, my father talks to me, in figures, about his new job in Arras, about his big office, about his staff of thirty-five, his three secretaries, his two official cars, his offset printing machine, about animals slaughtered because of foot and mouth disease, brucellosis or tuberculosis, slaughtered on the spot, buried in quicklime, swept away with bulldozers; he talks about his budget of millions for compensating the farmers. I am touched when he talks to me about little things, in the midst of this organization which seems as much to cripple him as to reassure him: about a ray of sunshine that comes through the blinds of his office every day at the same time, brushing his face. It amazes me that when he leaves he doesn't slip a hundred franc note into my hand with an apology.

Just before Easter: my father sends me an envelope containing two hundred francs 'to buy yourself some little nicknack'. Treacherously, I think that this money given by my father will be of use to me to buy a body, a sex.

Dinner with my mother. I didn't go to meet her off the train. I brought her a button to sew on. She had cottonwool in her ears. Just as she was leaving she told me 'You know I love you very much.' Over the meal she told me how when she got bored she would sleep in the afternoons so as to make it bearable, and she mimed the huddled-up way she slept, and several times in the muddle of her conversation she repeated the same odd-sounding words (excessive, abruptly shocking) about this sleep: 'refuge', 'oblivion'. I interjected with the news that this morning the wife of S., who works on the paper, threw herself under a metro train, and I couldn't but remark that she was the same age as my mother.

Memory of the accounts book that my father made my mother keep as a kind of humiliation (she took notes of things at the shops and then had to write down in the notebook all the food and household products she had bought, along with details of their prices).

With the passing years I at last find aspects of my mother in myself: she didn't like anyone mussing up her hair, she never went in swimming at the beach for fear of exposing her varicose veins, my father called her a stay-at-home, and her happy moments, like drunken raptures, sounded sudden false notes in the atonality of her behaviour. With the passing years there also came a resurgence of what my father had taught me: a timorous fearfulness, an extreme physical protectiveness.

A dream of breakdown resulting from the loss of three teeth in succession; I have the teeth in my hand, I'm looking at them, they are little pearly shells where, in a transparent liquid like seawater, there floats a small central membrane like lemon pulp. These shells are balanced in my hand and I'm afraid of their water and this substance spilling out of them. They fall from my hand and I feel doubly distraught by being unable to find them. I kill my sister with a knife and she immediately dies. My parents in turn want to kill me but I promise them I'll kill myself and they turn their attention to the body of my sister, to compose it and make up her face, and they succeed so well in recreating her appearance that she comes to life again; I wonder whether this murder is not a hoax they have played on me. On the ground I find my eyes, three crystalline blue shells which, as they fell, became embedded in a fragment of the floor which my brother-in-law begins to cut out to make a picture of it and give it to me, after protecting my eyes under a sheet of plastic that irritates me, that I want to peel away. Just before or after this I

am facing my parents, and am so distraught that I cry
and shake.

My mother describes the reception given by the Prefect,
with the President's wife: how she compares herself to
her. She bought herself an outfit in velvet and black silk
with matching shoes, and wore foundation make-up,
and even put on lipstick. She cleaned her rings, which
she couldn't get off her fingers, using a little mascara
brush.

Sunday afternoon: my mother's voice on the telephone
is probably the most annoying of intrusions.

Suzanne tells me how when my mother's in Paris she'll
point to some object or other (the little bronze Bacchus
for example) as if she wants it after her death. The first
thing I say to Suzanne is 'that's sordid', then I tell her
outright what I want, nothing to do with ownership (?),
which is to live in her apartment after her death. Then I
have second thoughts about what I said about my
mother, and I reproach myself. She is such a helpless
woman that owning things is her last resort. Then I
think that I myself am like capital for her, and that
children in general represent for their parents living
capital, which they manage, and this is weird because a

few days later I read an analogous observation in Kafka's *Journal*.

Yesterday, I tell my mother this in passing, over this lunch, surrounded by Suzanne and Louise, impassive spectators. Then my mother tells me for the first time that the nine months when she was expecting me were the most horrible in her life; it was my father who had pushed her into this pregnancy, after the painful birth of my sister, and during those nine months her hysterical wish was to get rid of me, she would fall downstairs deliberately so as to lose me. When I was finally extracted from her belly she implored: 'So long as he's dead! So long as he's stillborn!.' 'Then I saw you,' she said, 'all little and naked, pathetic, really pathetic, lying there on a table, and I screamed: be careful! he'll fall!'. . . Now my mother's eyes are filled with tears, and to distract attention from her feelings I ask Suzanne: 'What do you think of that, you, the cool one?', and Suzanne, instead of answering me, says to my mother: 'I think you've just made a declaration of love to your son . . .' Then my mother speaks about the relationship she had with me, 'this relationship that was . . .' and she falters searching for a word to qualify it. Louise, who so far had been silent, says: 'Carnal? . . .' My mother makes a feeble protest and Louise says: 'But carnal isn't necessarily to do with sex,' and I say that in fact I find this word very beautiful, very apt. Then I tell my mother: 'You were afraid that I'd fall off the table, but my body belongs to me completely, as far as I want to take it, and you have no right to identify with my nervous system; if tomorrow I want to let this body fall out of a window even, it's nothing to do with you . . .' I now realize the appalling harshness of these words. Then I tell my mother: 'I can't imagine anything crueller than having a child. If I had one I'd be even worse: I'd rape it, I'd kill it, I wouldn't let it get away from me . . .'

T. writes to his parents in Barcelona on his birthday: 'I thank you for having brought me into the world.' A gratitude which I lack.

The conversation between the mother and the son could have continued like this: 'I was naked and pathetic laid on that table, but tell me, did I already have this body? Might it not have been your contractions, your attempt at abortion, your going without food, your drunkenness which broke me, deformed me, made me concave like this? . . .'

Every time I see my mother I know she's going to talk about food, and it makes me despair.

My parents' new apartment, in Rochefort: built out of divided rooms, the partitions so thin you have to hold your breath so as not to be heard. The flaccidity of my prick. My instant disgust for certain objects (as well as for the gloomy light): the tin vase with the rose in it, the bathroom stool upholstered in mock blue fur and the bar of green soap that is for washing my genitals as well as theirs. My mother's constant jabbering, though I tell myself that this word-sickness is a sickness of solitude. My Dostoevskian repugnance for the way they whisper on the other side of my door in the morning, whispers that seem more violent than screams and which put thoughts of murder in my head . . . So many negative things recorded, yet I come back pleased with my stay.

When he leaves me my father hands me a cheque and says: 'Here, your shoes are such a sorry sight . . .'

When I was asking her about this my mother reminded me of something I'd completely forgotten, of which I have no memory, even though it dates from a time later than my earliest memories; I was three and twice a week she took me to an establishment where I was given ultraviolet treatment in the hope of building up my bone mass; I had all my clothes taken off and was fitted with little round goggles that competely blinded me so that the rays wouldn't burn my eyes; and I made a fuss and cried and was strapped onto the table to stop me from wriggling about; my mother had to hold my hand or stroke my hair. She describes this with a measure of pain in her voice, as if the memory of this scene has aroused her pity, and I in imagining it begin to feel pity for myself.

Munich. Last night I get back before T. and settle down to reading (*Madame Bovary*) in the hotel room but I fall asleep, I've left the bathroom light on and I wake with a start, seeing a silhouetted figure entering the room; I hear myself whisper 'Daddy' but it's T. that I see, and I'm at once disturbed by this, not that I associate T. with my father, but that sleep should return me to, surprise me in this infantile state . . .

I failed to show the slightest warmth today, or even familial courtesy, by not opening the door to my sister when she buzzed on the outside entryphone and I knew it was her, and by leaving my mother to go to the station all on her own with a heavy suitcase, and I'm almost ashamed of this lack of basic decency . . .

My cousin P. says: 'It's not photography that interests me, it's the image. Images. When I see you for example, I see an image, I see the image of your grandfather, Lucien Guibert, but I just can't get over the hair being added on,' and she lifts the fringe covering my forehead to confirm the truth of what she's saying.

The mother remembers the twenty-five roses that her son had sent her, with a telegram, after a gynaecological operation; she tells him, with great feeling, that she even kept the telegram and one of the twenty-five roses, dried, but he can't even remember this, and his mother's emotion is suddenly an irritant, he can't bring himself to turn and look at her and he doesn't move, his gaze obstinately lost in the void, his jaw clenched; those twenty-five roses seem to him now like a folly, as people are wont to say when they receive flowers; nowadays he wouldn't send more than ten, if that, and this figure of twenty-five, this quantity of roses sent to his mother now causes him retrospective embarrassment, like affection overdone.

In the letters to the father there'd be nothing but money matters, thank you notes, like this: 'Thank you for your cheque for five hundred francs which allowed me to buy myself three pairs of multi-coloured boxer shorts, some eau de toilette and a train ticket for the island of Elba . . .'

Home again. Hearing my father's voice on the phone and for the first time hearing the voice of an old man. Wanting to cry.

My mother's distress, relayed to me by Suzanne, on seeing no more articles by me in the paper for a time (my holiday period), as if these articles, and my name on a page with a 500,000 print run were the sole proof of my existence, as if reading these articles were the only contact they could have with me, short of speech. And this distress of my mother's has repercussions on my own distress, this disappearance of my name from the paper comes to seem to me like a failure. I imagine that if they did not have this impression of my name as a seat of authority, importance and power – sometimes it's alarming and worrying enough for them to see my name cut down to initials – they would be much less tolerant of my homosexuality, its starkness would in their eyes turn me into an asocial creature, lost and threatened. 'The death of one's parents,' says A., 'is the day when you are finally released from always having something to prove.'

I'm walking with my father on a country road. An aeroplane has become trapped in a gorge and is circling ceaselessly to the point where it can go no further and keeps on coming up against the side of the ravine, from which it cannot escape. The plane is bound to drop in the end, only a miracle could save it, but what? For the mountainside to open up? I get down on my knees to pray and I tell my father to do the same. But the plane crashes. We go down to the bottom of the ravine to see the result of the accident. But the plane isn't smashed up, it's sitting on the ground quite intact, only locked inside it is death and its doors won't open; a terrible silence has fallen.

Not ridiculing nor belittling my mother's sorrow (the news that her youngest brother is dying), not making a laughing stock of this drama she clutches at as if to inject life, through death, into her moribund life, and not picturing that bloated or skeletal body on a drip and doped up with morphine, with the liver swollen to three times its size, the colourless stools and the blackish urine, picturing that it's the little blonde boy in the photo, fishing bare-chested by the riverbank, that my mother had gone to give her hand to.

The moment comes when one's thoughts turn to cancer, as a possibility, as a necessity. In itself cancer is like a child at first.

H. tells me that nowadays doctors take polaroid photographs of cancers when they operate on them, and in these photos you can see magnificent shapes and colours, monstrous, sometimes hairy and with teeth, the evidence of a birthing.

Just what kind of hypocrisy is it that makes my mother's voice on the phone change from the simpering, almost ethereal, other-worldly sham of devotion that she puts on when she talks to me, to the pure (I mean purely abject) self-interest that's in it five minutes later when she calls my great-aunts to tell them: 'Well, make sure you vote for G. eh, don't make a mistake on the ballot paper? And if we had the bad luck to have M. voted in, you're to go straightaway to the bank and withdraw every penny, the accounts would be blocked.'

On 10 May 1981, around eight in the evening, my mother bursts into tears in front of her television set; there has just appeared on the screen, electronically composed as if thousands of voices had united to form an image, the face of the new president of the Republic.

All the same M.'s election is a piece of good luck for my mother. At last she'll be able to get her paws on that money that was unjustly denied her thirty years ago and which she's had her eye on ever since, probably praying for her aunt's speedy demise, all with the excuse of the great socialist-communist threat. This stay-at-home who never stirs to go anywhere is suddenly in Paris organizing some kind of repossession commando assault with good old Louise as her accomplice, forcing the hand of the miserly but fortunately powerless Suzanne. There are the purses with gold coins in them, the ingots wrapped in old newspaper, the diamonds and emeralds in their little jewel boxes, all the booty laid out on the kitchen table up there on the third floor. My mother, who has taken charge of the share-out operation, ably rehearsed in advance, makes sure she gives herself the best share: after all, isn't she the favourite niece, well-nigh the adopted child of Suzanne and Louise? So the share-out takes place after her depradations, and the aunts are made to swear they'll never speak a word of it to the children; after all, isn't it all for them – we're really not that interested for ourselves – above all they musn't be told, they're still so thoughtless, they have no idea of the value of money, we can't even trust them with the share we promised to let them have, they're so hopeless they would blow it all . . . At the same time my mother loads up the silverware.

A few months later my mother writes a letter to Suzanne to tell her that 'the time has come to tighten our belts'; from now on she will no longer call her on Sunday mornings to hear her news as she had done regularly for fifteen years. A stamp is cheaper than a long-distance phone call to Paris. She takes this opportunity to complain that the gold is clogged up with earth.

Suzanne, who relates this to me with delighted consternation, tells me the story of this gold that has been held by the family over several generations like a cross; it was bought cheaply by her husband, then hidden in several stone pots that were buried in trenches, then dug up, the pots smashed with pick-axes and the gold sliding into the earth; hands had to be dirtied to loosen the clods of earth, the gold travelled far, across wars and roadblocks, it filled the pockets of my mother's brothers, two little boys who passed right under the Germans' noses like flowers, at Montparnasse station. The only pleasure this gold has ever given is the pleasure of burying it.

These extorted diamonds, these purses full of gold have to be carefully hidden, dispersed, their value scattered through the whole apartment, under a broken flagstone in the kitchen, at the very back of cupboards, knotted into rags, places no one could think of. The silverware is crammed into a box stuck out in a corridor and covered with newspaper. Only once my mother unearthed and reassembled the scattered items, spreading them out before her as if to feed on them, as if to draw warmth from them; she would like the fire of the stones to blind her and the metal to flow, but she knows she has become the mistress of the coldest treasure on earth, a treasure mute and unyielding, poisonous, no longer with a story to tell and, like the nasty little Vitafor cross, chilling the skin the moment it's worn; there's no longer any good in feeling it or counting it, she would have to be able to put it in her mouth and swallow it, choke on it, and then excrete it and in the nubbly faeces find the nuggets of it, have the pearls wound in the necklaces of intestines, and rub her little lips with a precious stone. It is not so, balefully she contemplates this treasure that has come too late, she does not lie down naked on it, more likely it would cover her up and bury her. Why then doesn't she chuck it into the rubbish chute?

Meet my mother on a bus. She has come to Paris to have a skin biopsy, a test for a possible cancer. Hardening of the tissue.

I dream I'm in a market where two evil-doers waylay me, surround me and put a knife to my throat, sticking it in a little to frighten me; I empty my pockets for them, there's a little money, but out of malevolence the one holding the knife slashes it slowly across the surface of my skin all the way from my nose to my ear right below my eye. My thoughts are: a gash, a scar, they're getting away, what am I to do? Keep the gash, a red mark that doesn't bleed (I can see the scar it will leave) or have it erased? My father comes to my aid. I'm lying flat on my stomach on a bed and I want him to fuck me; he comes up behind me and as he penetrates me he says: 'He who has his bum filled is damned' and he gives a little laugh as he says it, as if to turn me on. While he's fucking me (he does it a bit like T.) I touch his belly, which isn't all that fat. Then my mother knocks on the door and gets cross, for my father has locked the door, just as he did to screw my mother when I was at school; my father panics about being discovered, I wake up.

I'm really afraid that my mother will bury herself alive, that she'll set to throwing earth over herself to cover herself up; this earth could be her cutting herself off more and more from the world, her getting angry with her children, or it could even be that hardening of the tissue which she has provoked to eat away her skin.

My mother's hysteria over lunch when she sees my hands: 'You've got purple nails! You've got purple nails!' I answer: 'You get on my nerves.'

A bargain, with my parents, a blackmail: now you must buy my life, day after day, for I want to be a crippled child.

Incapacity to show my mother any warmth.

The father (to the mother): 'How did we manage to make a big boy like that?' and he slips a fifty franc note into his son's hand.

In Athens, on the evening of 6th September 1981, without knowing why, I write these words:

The woman is naked beneath her fur coat, which she draws open slightly as the cars go by. Something whitish and rounded is outlined between the two beaver panels, a soft, luxuriant fur, a little worn, no smoothness, no sheen, no roughness, perhaps a breast or the curve of the stomach, a faint white flash half glimpsed inside the drab brown fur; the tuft of red hairs is sucked into the shadow, one hand in a pocket holds the coat forward and, as some of the cars go by, moves wider to let in the air, to ventilate, it's midwinter. My father's car, the old Rover 90 which he bought second hand for two thousand francs, brakes alongside the woman, his suede jacket thrown onto the back seat; he winds down his window and leans out to take a closer look at her; she moves a bit closer to the car and he shoots off again, zooming around the block three times, then disappears.

My mother has a mastectomy.

First letter to my mother.

I'm in Athens. On the day of the operation, the seventh (afterwards I feel bad about having said it was 'a good day' to boost her morale), I'm superstitious; I touch wood without warning whenever someone speaks to me. I'm afraid, but it's an abstract fear which is barely conscious, I don't imagine things. In the evening I am uncertain whether to telephone for news and in the end decide not to. The next morning I make the effort to call, on that black bakelite telephone, and I'm relieved – simultaneously anxious and relieved that I can't get through – the line to France is permanently engaged. I go to a painter's studio and he shows me some female nudes; there's a lot of violence in these paintings, not just a painterly intoxication but an erotic fury, big vicious brush strokes. I remember that two days earlier I've written the word breast in a text and it's a word that I never write, that I keep well away from my fingers. When I get back from the painter's studio I dial the number again and since I still can't get through one of the two women who are with me dials the number for me, as if relieving me of something painful. Finally she holds out the receiver: it's ringing, someone lifts the phone, I hear the voice of Louise and straight away she speaks the most piercing words I've ever had said to me: 'Your mother was operated on yesterday, she had a breast taken off,' and in that moment I drop the phone and it's as if something was abruptly being sliced off my body, as if I was being atrociously hurt through an assault on the flesh that had given me my flesh, the breast that had furnished my life. I sob, I moan, I scream, I'm like a lost child far from my mother; I feel

the hands of the two women who are there gently
stroking my hair. I lift the phone again and hear
something even more terrible: she doesn't know
about this terribly intimate thing that's happened to
her body, it's being kept from her, to spare her, and I
am to know it in her stead, and in this absurd
displacement of awareness it feels as if I am in my turn
undergoing the surgery, with no anaesthetic, it's upon
me that the wound is imprinted and I daren't imagine
it. I daren't imagine the redness there, and the dressing, and also the flesh that's been removed and lifted
away, perhaps dissected, the nipple lost, screwed up in
a bag somewhere, shrivelled and bloody. I pack my
bags right away for the plane. In the airport lounge I
run into Moustapha, a boy I run into about every
couple of years and whom I'm always glad to see
again, then lose touch with. He's going back in a
hurry too, after a phone call, because his sister has
been operated on for a tumour and she's unconscious.
For my mother he gives me a little carpet he's bought
on one of the islands, and the drachmas he has left
over. On the plane I sit apart from him to write to
my mother; it's the first time I've ever written to her
and afterwards it strikes me as appalling that she has
to have a part of herself amputated before I can give
her proof of my love. I tell her that I shall love her
more, that I do love her more, but the next day I'm

horrified when I think of what that means: die and I'll love you even more, you know.

I take a taxi from the airport and get to the hospital. It's dark by now. I walk around the building and see a lift cage, transparent, with lights on; I can make out small silhouetted figures going down in it, among whom I can recognize my father. Through the frosted windowpane of the hospital rooms I try to make out a shadow that might be my mother. Now, out of breath, I climb the stairs, with my luggage and carrying the little painting that the painter K. gave me, though I don't know what it is yet, for I haven't unwrapped it. I knock on door 214 and my father and mother loom up behind me in the corridor, holding a catheter full of urine; she's unsteady on her feet, he's supporting her. For the first time now I see a very old woman with a yellow complexion and pinched lips. My father puts her to bed and I take her in my arms as I have never done, holding her close for a long time, with no disgust, my disgust for her is gone now. I give her my letter and make the effort to give her a lively account of my trip. I unwrap the picture to take my first look at it along with them; it's very fine, luminous. It's of a young bricklayer naked from the waist up, holding a plumb-line.

★

This woman who has never written in her life except for letters has begun to write, to keep her journal, describing every single occurrence of her life in the hospital, every single time someone steps into her room, every single occasion when a finger is laid on her body. She wrote right up until the anaesthetic, when torpor completely blurred the clumsy strokes of the letters; she wrote 'happy birthday' to her husband, for her operation fell on the same day. Beforehand she had asked him to throw the roses he had bought her into her coffin.

My mother turns slightly in her bed and where her nightdress is loose I see a strip of cotton bandage crosswise under her arm, which she complains about a great deal, as if it had been twisted during the operation. Before we leave, while I'm there, she asks my father to rub her back with a massage glove, and I discover a very pretty back, or else I'm rediscovering the back of a very young woman. At night I can't turn onto my right side, the side that's painful for her, it's painful for me too.

In the evening I go out for dinner with my father. In the taxi going along boulevard du Montparnasse he points out a café where he went once with my mother before they were married and tells me how he then saw her home, 'on his best behaviour' back to her aunts' pharmacy. I try not to let him see that I find this youthful memory very painful. We go and say hello to Suzanne and Louise, who is always a bird of ill omen and tells us gleefully that a man in a circus has been eaten by a lion. We have dinner at the Taverne Alsacienne, my father has a choucroute and I have oysters and munster cheese.

My mother clasps my letter to her wound as if through the dressing the words could penetrate and cauterize it.

My father now calls my mother: 'My Amazon, my little girl, my kitten, my little doll', but she's a little doll he would also like to wrap in a shroud of sweetness (I can't stand how at the florist's the salesgirl lays the flowers flat on the paper then encloses them in a kind of cellophane vacuum; each staple she punches in is a nail hammered into wood).

She says her body, her skin are now made of cardboard.

I must say that I expected this cancer; it's in the logic of my mother's history. It's ten, twenty years now (hard to know exactly how it started) that my mother has been worrying, fretting and biting her lip. Cancer is just subsidized suicide, acceptable (for misfortune enhances the value of life), taken care of by the National Health.

My mother says she has been happy, that my father made her happy, that he never hit her; she says she has never had any personality, that she's lazy and when she's feeling low she sleeps.

As my mother recovers, traces of irritation and dislike begin to creep back into my relationship with her.

She says she can smell blood, repeats that her body is made of cardboard.

The woman who smiles every time she wants to weep.

The heat in the hospital room makes me sleepy, my heart beats faster and my mother lists what she gets for her meals.

My mother's got a bellyful of shit (to fight her constipation she is given jam that tastes of redcurrants). She talks like a little girl, claiming marks for good behaviour because she manages to raise her arm a little higher every day. She weeps. She has asked for a new dressing even though her last stitches have been taken out today; she can't bear to look at herself without a dressing and asked for a young man, an intern, to be taken out of the room once her top half was naked (a new focus for our shared distress). When I look at her I feel like a dead weight, a deadening rather than an enlivening presence; I already regret this, but there's nothing I can do.

I know that my mother would like me to rub her back with a massage glove and eau de Cologne as my father does when he's there; she hints at this, saying it in a roundabout way, but there is no way that I can comply with her request.

The mother who tries to show her wound to her son.

The father who tells his son: 'I'm a nonentity.'

Black marks crisscrossing my mother's upper body, squares and dots, like a landing strip.

The new bedroom, light and airy; the introduction of light making the situation bearable (no longer the cavernous light of the hospital)

The suicide, the son of the condemned woman, had left this note: 'I don't want to know if my mother's going to live or die; I don't want this suspense, I want neither hope nor despair.'

The mother's suffering: she weeps into my ear on the phone.

The mother who says: 'We aren't old, we still make love.'

The mother describing her nightmares (the nurse binding her toes while the doctor stubs out a cigarette on her arm).

The father visiting his son, who is unaccustomed to seeing him, least of all at home. He asks to go to the toilet and is away for five minutes. He comes back all flustered saying: 'I couldn't do it, it must be the state I'm in.'

I've decided to give my mother a white blouse for Christmas, but even before I buy it, even before I pick it out, I become afraid she'll want to wear this white blouse in her grave.

My skin's burning, like my mother's, burnt with the radiation treatment.

This evening the first dinner out in town with my mother. My mother like a poor timid thing unadapted to life (and me?).

Dream that I find my mother hanged, but it's exhaustion that's left her hanging in space and when I shake her she comes round. She says she wants to go for a walk with me on the rocks. We're at Croix-de-Vie.

Struck by the fact that Suzanne, for all her intelligence and independence, should have given in to the narrow-minded money ethic by sharing out all she owned six months earlier without a word to me, between her nieces and nephews who are hated by her and whose greed and pettiness she well knows.

My mother asks me for a photo of the fog.

My mother on the phone: her poor dying voice.

The nurse massaging my mother's arm to bring back the circulation.

A nightmare about my mother's death followed by a nightmare about stringy meat. Then the pleasure of being beaten by T. in the dream after that. My dreams are orders.

My mother's voice in my dream, and me keeping my sobs from her.

In the hotel room in Cannes I try to make myself come in the most unlikely way: sitting in front of the television, looking at a woman's bosom (isn't my mother dying there), eating a piece of bread with too-sweet strawberry jam on it.

My mother's face puffed up with cortisone, a bit like a mastiff's head; I hate her so much.

Disgust for my mother's letter, which I tear up immediately. But I'm afraid that I'll have to look for the pieces in the waste basket when I get back from my trip.

In my dream I'm at Croix-de-Vie with my mother, and I take her to see the Trou du Diable.

Dream of my father coming home in the evening to tuck me into bed with some tender words; happiness resurrected, but I'm the same age as I am now, and at the same time I'm thinking in my dream that they've won, these parents of mine, because after what will seem like a time when I've gone astray I've returned on my own to my prison. Later, in the morning, dream of a large man's corpse floating face down and ashen by the shore, near where people are swimming. A woman alone in the back of a boat, his wife perhaps, manoeuvring the helm to get closer to the body.

A note written after a gap of three weeks; the too emotional lunch with my mother. Because she believes she's going to die and that she's back in Paris for one last time to see her children, though she doesn't say it. Because she tells me: 'You know, I'm very proud of you and the choices you've made in your life, and your courage and the way you bear being on your own.' And because it's when she's on the threshold as we're parting that she starts blurting out, like a throwaway remark, what she held back all through lunch, what she stopped short of saying soberly, perhaps if I don't say it now I shall never be able to say it: 'I would so much love to be lying on your bed, silently, without stirring, so as not to disturb you, while you write in the next room . . .' Feelings that are almost unbearable.

The day of my mother's operation: flesh being removed.

Dream that I'm caressing the nipples of a supine woman whose breasts have no thickness.

A visit to the parents. I let myself in for it one afternoon the month before, when in a moment of short-lived exhilaration I'd made up my mind not to back out at the last moment, whatever my fears, dread or feverishness. I come home feeling deeply upset, shaken by this specimen of human misery, it would probably be better to see half-alive rotted flesh in a hospital bed, it would be less pitiful. Everything that's been most awful and petty in myself seems to have been inherited from them. My mother's suspicious and exasperating vitality, for all her two whittled down breasts, which only death will be able to silence. The ugliness and triviality to which they've mortgaged their life. It's not only them I detest, along with my detestation, but I detest what they look at and what they eat, I detest the seats they sit on and the clothes that cover their bodies, I detest their apartment, I detest what they read, I detest their fear (and I write these dreadful things listening to music as cheerful as water running on a well-oiled surface), I detest their furniture, I detest their frozen food. They come to pick me up at the station, in the café my father gathers the sugar lumps that are in the saucers and puts them in his pocket for the dog he'll see at the restaurant the next day. The sugar is put away in an old jam pot, the waste paper baskets are made from plastic water bottles cut in half, and my mother squats down inside a cupboard to show me a box with a new set of crockery that they've bought. She doesn't show me the little nest-egg of diamonds, emeralds, rubies and gold bars that must be hidden away in some wretched nook or cranny. From the window she shows me a ghastly mud-covered expanse with electric pylons and tower blocks like rat cages and the main highway running past it and she tells me: 'You see, it's nice, there's no one overlooking us.' In the evening my father parks the car below their windows because one night someone syphoned off his petrol, and my mother sleeps with one eye open for thieves. She sees children playing ball on the waste ground and she tells my father nastily: 'One day they're going to break the car windows!' I'm almost happy when she says she's in pain, I'm almost happy when I see the horribly high-coloured puffiness of her skin, her fat rear end in her tight trousers. I've been in enough pain myself all the sleepless night long, dreaming that I heaped abuse on them, one after the other; I tossed and turned in pain and was afraid of crying out, ready to stuff the sheet in my mouth to stop myself from coughing, for I could hear my father prowling about on the other side of my door to offer me a blanket. They appear before me in quilted nylon dressing gowns; Louise has had me bring them a selection of tins of *pâté de foie gras* and for our meal my mother has selected the plainest one. On the train going there, in a sweat of apprehension, all I did was go back over some of their past lies and mean tricks, despite myself, for they came back to me unbidden. On the return journey I only carry regrets for a visit that has done nothing but offer them an image of their desolation and heighten my resentment, adding these unpleasant pages to my journal. I go home with the certainty of never having to see them again unless on their death bed, but maybe I will die before them.

When I get to the station they take me for a walk along the banks of the Sèvre Niortiase; it's cold, the boats are deserted, I walk between the two of them and, just as happens to me in museums, I get a phenomenal erection, an embarrassment, a cramp that almost stops me from walking and which I try to hide from them by gathering my coat over it with my hands in my pockets. I'm afraid that this hanged man's erection won't leave me the whole while I'm with them.

She's chosen two books from the mail order catalogue, the ones whose covers are reproduced biggest and are at the front. She only goes into town to check in a bookshop that she has paid thirty francs less for the same books.

Their stinginess has reached such a point that if a circular told them: there's a discount you can have on your water bill, but we'll supply you with a type of water that makes your gums bleed, tick this box if you want the discount, then they would tick it.

With a lie – that he has to drop in to read over a letter his secretary has typed for the mayor – my father gets me into his office, the director's office with its leather upholstered door; he settles proudly into his armchair and waves my mother and myself to sit down across from him: he comes across a mistake and corrects it with a snide dig at his secretary, then takes the blotter stamp to dry the ink. My mother casts her eyes around the room and remarks to me with satisfaction: 'It's big, eh, it's big don't you think?' I reply: 'Yes, it's big.' Then she looks up and stares at the ceiling, saying: 'I wonder what those little black spots can be inside the lampshades, they must be cockroaches, what do you think?' I reply: 'Yes, they must be cockroaches.' My father gets up and goes over to unlock a little cupboard, giving a glimpse of two bottles of champagne.

Start of a novel to be called *My Parents* (rather in the style of Emmanuel Bove) which would begin thus: Now that my parents are dead thank God (but I'm lying) I am able to write everything bad that I think of them or have thought of them, only praying to heaven never to give me such a spiteful and ungrateful son.

★

The father comes by to visit his son, but it isn't even a visit, he just comes by to pick up the record player he'd given his son for his twelfth birthday; he was set on getting the old heap back now that his son had at long last made up his mind after fifteen years to buy a new 'system'. The father came all the way from Niort to Paris to get the machine, which can barely make the records rotate and which gives Callas a baritone voice. He enters his son's flat, once again looks at things without seeing them, his eyes gliding over the stuffed owl on the mantelpiece but stopping at the banana tree in the corner. I say: 'It's a banana tree.' Then he says, in utter seriousness, as if making an urgent, important request: 'So it's a banana tree, well when you come and see us will you be so good as to bring some bananas?' I say: 'How can I, it doesn't bear fruit, they can't bear fruit here.' And, quite distraught at this, my father repeats: 'So it can't bear fruit' then he leaves straight away, turning on his heel, weighed down with the record player.

Alone, I'm disheartened by these remarks, which are just one link in the long chain of outrageous meanness glimpsed the weekend before (getting bananas 'for free'), but they make me so sad that they go beyond meanness. Of course it's me, the barren tree, who cannot bear fruit. And that's the deeper motive for taking back the wreck of a machine: taking back from the sterile son what should never have been given to him, since he has given nothing in return, since he has short-circuited the current of life. A sadness full of pathos.

Insomnia: a child crying in the night upset by a nightmare and calling for his daddy; in this room that's usually undisturbed by outside noise I am appalled by the memory of my own childhood panics and the soothing hands and voice of my father, of my mother. A somewhat painful shame at my detachment and feelings of ingratitude.

She teaches her husband to iron for the time when she's dead. And as I tidy up this sad afternoon I throw away the notes from her that I come across (I read them again first, but their housewifely affection seems so paltry).

Dream of the father, an old man, leaving the mother to go around the world alone with an empty black satchel open in his hand.

Mother making an effort to put on an animated voice on the phone, and me as if I'm making an effort to put on an afflicted voice.

The mother on the telephone: like an animal cowering at the back of its lair to die. She says she can't hold a book any more, it hurts too much (haunted by the idea of shame for the preceding notes).

The death of the body, death of pleasure, death of emotion, death of adventure, death of writing, the imminent death of the mother.

In the city the father and his son happen to go past some bare railings, almost invisible in the dark, while the mother is dying far away in her bed in the provinces; he says: 'That's where I kissed your mother for the first time, that's where we did our dissecting, I plunged right in, kissed her and said: what the hell.'

On the phone the mother says that the day before, around Angoulême, through the rain-spattered windows of the car she saw the façade of a château, flat and with no interior, just a baroque façade with statues, the sky to be seen through its windows.

The same old tragedy: congenital inheritance (the origin of suffering); the discovery of this kidney defect.

Thinking back on the revolver that was shut away in the metal box at the top of my father's cupboard, I wonder if this revolver still exists, still belongs to them, whether my mother could get her hands on it (what a murderer I make) . . .

I always think of my mother when I'm on a plane, in a window seat. But it's because my eyes are seeing what she has never seen.

Mother the unbeliever, who's going to go to Lourdes to expose her two pared-down breasts in the grotto: will they grow again?

Sudden memory of the little knob of flesh at the base of my spine – a peculiarity I shared with my father – that as an adolescent I twice desperately tried to have operated on.

Memory of kissing my mother for the last time: her cheek smelled of ether.

The surprise of seeing that my father was Kafka's contemporary for the first three years of his life: this brings me closer to him.

My feet are still on fire and for the first time, today, because of them, though I know I'll never be able to admit it to him, I miss my father, dreadfully; the slightest soreness, the least scratch and my feet would be in his lap, hardly belonging to me any more; I left it up to him, his hands were soft, to the point of being off-putting, and now that with this cursed fungus my feet have never hurt so badly, I long, desperately, to put them in his hands. I wonder how much stronger or more painful this longing would be were he dead.

Mother calls to say that something strange happened the day before: between nine and ten in the morning she could smell me, she smelled my odour, then the odour went away (you don't have to define this odour or ask her to define it, its content has to be unspeakable: is it a stink of goat or a smell of shellfish, is it as wood odour or a sex odour, a smell of wool or of infant diarrhoea?).

Return from New York. My mother's dying voice.

Lunch with father. While he's eating he makes a note of what it is in a notebook.

Father saying: 'You're less scruffy than usual.'

The father's crazy behaviour; he can't stand being away from work, yet for no good reason, just to escape his wife, gets on a train. The endless vampirism of the couple: a struggle to the death.

Dream that the schoolboys of this very cold region have to bandage their hands, and that the tips of their fingers burst out through the open frettings of the bandage (yesterday my mother said that this was how it was with her skin).

They take blood from my mother's groin because they can get no more blood out of her arm.

Return from Egypt. Mother's voice on the phone echoing through the empty flat that has just been cleared for removal; she says: 'I'm cured of my cancer.'

My mother being sorry that I've had my hair cut.

Seeing me with my new haircut my father sees his father again. Dolefully he tells me, as if as a result I was the one being reproached: 'He never bought me the motorbike he promised me . . .'

With Suzanne's biggest diamond my father has bought himself a new sailing boat, one bigger than the *Doher*. My mother rings me to ask a favour: she's read in the paper that there's a Soviet company on at a Paris theatre with a show called *Avos and Jono*; she had some idea that *Avos* meant hope in Russian and she asks me to check this out. First I ask a friend on the paper who's just been the Moscow correspondent for two years and he confesses that he's already forgotten the meaning of this word, common though it is. I ring the theatre to ask the same question and I'm told that *Avos* is the name of a ship, but as for the meaning of the word the theatre man is in the dark. I wind up going to the Soviet bookshop in rue de Buci and a young woman assures me that *Avos* just means *perhaps*. I phone this to my mother, who retorts: 'Oh, so it isn't *hope* then, it's *perhaps*, but that's perfectly all right.' My father has to transport the *Avos* from the shipyard near Marseilles, where it has been built, to the harbour of Port-Gos, where a berth has been leased for ninety-nine years. My father tells me on the phone that he transported the boat 'with a pal' and he puts such delighted emphasis on this word that I instantly come to the sad conclusion that this man is a professional transporter who did it for a fee.

Dream of some amorous encounter from my youth which my memory has blocked out completely: I am back in the place where it happened, now all in ruins (a structure has collapsed). It seems I've been here with a lover, here on this bench where I'm sitting, and have taken his hands, have kissed his lips, how can I know for sure? So who would this lover have been and where would this episode be? Where in relation to other loves?

But it turns out that it belongs not to my past but my father's as if there were one single unique memory that I shared with my father . . .

My love for Suzanne must be dreadful for my mother: the idea that on top of everything else – her life, her happiness – Suzanne has also stolen her children.

My mother's shock after I made up my mind to own up to my material difficulties.

T. bathes me in the sea; I cling to him like a crippled child in the arms of his father.

I feel that when T. comes back into the living-room on the last evening, it's like a father too, putting a son to bed or checking that he's well tucked in: he whisks the duvet away from my naked body and it's still as a father that he jerks me off, kisses me and bruisingly kneads my breast: rising up above me, imperiously untouchable, full of kindness for the disabled son.

T. is licking my bum as I talk to my father on the phone; he's at the Gare de Lyon, rushing to catch a train back to my mother.

Another proof of my parents' baseness (the money they demand from Suzanne to bury my father's mother). Don't let them get away with anything.

The father going to photograph his mother's decaying body, as if he were 'on the scrounge' yet again. Looking in the mirror to shave, the first thought that is stirred in me for this woman on the news of her death: that this woman lived only in and for the expectation that her son would come scrounging.

My father: when we end up alone in the garden he loosens his clothes and twists at where his jacket buttons up as if he were wringing it out, then he points at the buckle holes in his belt to show how far his body has separated from his clothes.

Naked in the hands of T., fucking me, bathing me, soaping my head and cutting my hair, like a daddy. T. brings me back to life.

Wonderful dinner with father on the night of departure: so many things to tell that I put them aside for now.

My mother goes to the station to meet Abbé Herniot arriving from Courlandon; he's wearing a soutane; he changes out of it in a café toilet; he reappears in layman's clothes; they spend the morning in a hotel; he changes back again in another café after they leave the hotel; they go to have lunch at Suzanne's with her and her husband, who has never got wind of what's going on. One day my mother has to tell her aunt everything: that she goes to bed with this Abbé, that she steals money from her to give it to him, but the Abbé has just upped the rate of his blackmail and she doesn't want to see him again, ever. It's my great-aunt who opens the door to the Abbé for that last time, while my mother, tearful in her room, will have been watching for his arrival from behind the curtain: 'Never set foot in this house again,' Suzanne tells him.

At the very same time my father is getting himself thrown out of the house in Nice where he's a frequent visitor. While the young woman weeps in her room her parents tell him: 'She doesn't want to see you any more, you've made her too unhappy, don't come here again.' He had gone to collect her to go to the opera; the family has a perennial subscription to the same box. My father goes anyway in the hope of finding her there; an Italian company is doing *Madame Butterfly*. Its music and its story tear my father's heart: it dawns on him for the first time that he's in love with the young woman, that he only goes out of his way to make her unhappy so as to cure himself of this love, out of fear of marriage, with the excuse of an erroneous and indiscreet diagnosis by the young woman's doctor, who is also a friend of his: 'If you marry her you'll be nursing her for the rest of your life.' My father takes up with the young woman and her household once more, but the same obsessive fears assail him again, he becomes hateful towards her again; on the eve of their engagement he runs into a girl in the street with whom he begins, as if with calculation, an increasingly passionate relationship which makes him increasingly lukewarm and edgy with his fiancée. My father tells me this story over the wonderful dinner of 15th December 1984 where for the first time in more than fifteen years we become friends again; he wasn't sent packing because he was blackmailing this bourgeois household as Suzanne had told me; it was simply that the wedding didn't take place; for the second time, but this time it was final, and he stopped going to the house. He stayed on a bit longer in Nice, had several mistresses and was snubbed by the young woman whenever he ran into her. Then he says to me: 'You're finally going to know why your name is Hervé: because of a Monsieur Hervé who was very seductive.' I ask my father: 'Were you attracted to men too?' And he answers, with a trace of embarrassment: 'Not attracted, rather the opposite, I felt something more like disgust,' and he adds, so as not to bring me down: 'But it's only a matter of hormones . . .'

One evening he makes the acquaintance of this seductive Monsieur Hervé (it still amuses me to recall that when I was a child the shopkeeper would call my mother Madame Hervé) who, in the course of their conversation tells him: 'Liquidate all your assets, sell your surgery, your horses, your sailing boat, change it all into gold and don't tell a soul, and I'll make you your fortune in South America; I'll have you embark at Tangiers, you'll strike it rich . . .' For a few months my father goes on seeing this Monsieur Hervé just to fine-tune the plan, tempted by this flight, lucidly hopeful for a better world that might just as well be South America as the one you get to by cutting your own throat; my father knows the risk he is running and it's perhaps this which is most seductive. As Monsieur Hervé advised, he finds a buyer for his surgery, turns over his two horses to a film company's stables, sells off his Ford and his sailing boat, and converts all this money into gold. But at the very time when he's to meet Monsieur Hervé, instead of going to the appointment he gets on a train for Paris. He decides to go back to his medical studies. With every week that goes by he sees the gold melt away between his fingers; he goes to the gold exchange to hand over one coin after another for a small sum of money that is gobbled up in no time. And it is this obsessive fear of losing money, he confides, that makes it impossible for him to be contented with this cursed gold, come too late, that he has gone to such lengths to bury somewhere or other, and which will disappear in a landslide. It is because he can now no longer change it for money, and having not a penny left to his name, that he will try one last time to scrounge from Suzanne so as to bury his mother's corpse.

The father who sometimes lies down on his mother's bed, just to look at what she looked at, a small section of ceiling.

The mother who complains about the the dryness of her eyes: in the morning the eyelid won't come unstuck from the eye; she bathes it in camomile.

The father has come back alone to his mother's house to do an inventory of the furniture. Snow has brought his car to a standstill, the boiler has frozen, the radiator pipes have burst and water has come through one of the ceilings and is lying stagnant over a table. My father turns on the gas cooker and leaves the flame burning, he plugs in the only electric fire; he sees that he has managed to bring the indoor temperature up to just above freezing, it's twelve below outside. He has put on five sweaters, worn-out old things of his mother's, and to make up his bed has heaped up all the blankets and duvets in the house. He has a futile wait for someone to come and repair the boiler, and waits for the notary to call him to make the appointment for the inventory. But nobody's stirring in this weather. He goes out to walk to the local highways department to ask for the free bag of salt to which he's entitled, which will be given to him on sight of an electricity bill, and which he will sprinkle on the road outside the house.

But the father says that the cold is fine for him, that it takes him back to that time of his adolescence when he was happy, to the days of winter sports in an unheated chalet.

When, for the first time, after a wait of so many years, the mother will finally be able to see her son on television, at the very moment when he's about to come on, without even a whimper, the picture dwindles to nothing, and her long wait is reduced to that tiny fluorescent dot, that infuriating point which no scream, no blow, no tears of entreaty can reanimate; the white dot is no more than a memory of light; her son is there behind the black screen with its convex glass; she was so angry.

Today the father says that he has destroyed all the photos and correspondence of his uncle Raoul, whom he truly adored, and who was a great artist; he has only kept, by chance in one of his pockets, a single letter of his, written in the sanatorium, beginning: 'My darling love.' He tells me that one day he will show me this letter. He tells me that when he was fifteen he often went to this hospital to be examined, convinced that he, like this uncle whom he loved so much, had tuberculosis. Inside my head I can feel the abscesses that destroyed M.'s brain; they hurt.

The mother's voice on the phone denudes her of her flesh, dematerializes her woman's body, obliterates simultaneously her ageing and my disgust; reduces her, beyond all distance or any death, to a compass of affection, to a golden measure of maternal flux, like a telepathic umbilical cord.

My father asks me if I've got any ideas about him taking up some kind of work. He tells me he's thought of being a book dealer (with the death of his aunt he's just brought home several cases of books which belonged to the famous uncle), we could open a little bookshop together. He asks me if I've got time to go with him to the shop where decorations are sold; he wants to buy himself a spare for his rosette as Officer of Merit in agriculture. I ask him why this decoration matters to him and he tells me: 'It's the proof that I've done my job well for thirty years.'

Why didn't my father also destroy the books that belonged to his uncle Raoul, since he thought that books could spread diseases?

My mother dreams that she went with me as an adult to look for me as a little boy: that together we ask people whether they've seen this child go by, ask the woman in the café whether he's been there demanding a lemonade, ask the horses on the merry-go-round whether he's ridden them, ask the waves whether he's drowned.

The hatred of this book's dedication was of course fictitious.

The father set sail and gave himself up to the storm, his rosary around his neck. His flesh was stripped away. A skeleton steered his boat, with a rosary as scarf.